"Why are you s   Reid Cavanaugh money?"

Chloe persisted with her questions. "It's not as if he's a charity case. What did you do anyway— embezzle it?"

"Hardly," Cassidy said. "I told you—it was a loan."

"Then why go to such lengths to pay it back? A personal check would do the same thing."

"But if he doesn't cash a check, the money stays in my account. This way, even if he tears up the money order, it's like he's destroying hundred-dollar bills."

Chloe pounced. "And why would he want to tear it up?"

"Oh, for heaven's sake, Chloe—next you'll be thinking I'm being blackmailed."

Chloe's eyes brightened. "Are you? Though I can't think what you could be blackmailed for— you're so pure you could compete in the Miss America pageant!"

Leigh Michaels had plans to be the world's best feature-writing newspaper reporter when she graduated at the top of her class from Drake University's School of Journalism. But other things intervened, and instead she worked in radio, in public relations and as a reference librarian before starting to write romance novels.

But she doesn't see her career as a big change from her original plans. ''I still investigate things and report them,'' she says. ''I still dig into people and find out what makes them tick. And if one of my heroines turns out to be the editor of *Time* someday, I'll have all the fun of holding that job, and none of the actual work!''

Books by Leigh Michaels

Don't miss any of our special offers. Write to us at the following address for information on our newest releases.

Harlequin Reader Service
P.O. Box 1397, Buffalo, NY 14240
Canadian address: P.O. Box 603,
Fort Erie, Ont. L2A 5X3

PROMISE ME TOMORROW

Leigh Michaels

Harlequin Books

TORONTO • NEW YORK • LONDON
AMSTERDAM • PARIS • SYDNEY • HAMBURG
STOCKHOLM • ATHENS • TOKYO • MILAN

Original hardcover edition published in 1990
by Mills & Boon Limited

ISBN 0-373-03141-6

Harlequin Romance first edition August 1991

PROMISE ME TOMORROW

CHAPTER ONE

SUNSHINE poured in the big window at the top of the long staircase, but the halls of the big old frame house were still quiet. The girls who had not been able to avoid scheduling eight o'clock classes were already on campus, and most of the rest were—as usual—still asleep when Cassidy Adams emerged from the tiny two-room apartment reserved for the sorority's house-mother and descended to the dining-room.

A senior girl wearing a designer ensemble, her make-up self-consciously perfect, looked up from her dis-pirited inspection of a slice of dry wholewheat toast and groaned.

'And it's not even Monday,' Cassidy murmured. She poured herself a cup of coffee from the carafe on the sideboard. 'So what's the problem, Heather?'

'You.'

'Already?' It was light. 'And I've only just got up.' Cassidy filled a small dish with fresh fruit, put two bran muffins on a plate, and sat down at the head of the table.

'That's what's bothering me. Every girl in this sorority spends half the day trying to look her best, and in five minutes in the morning you put us all to shame. It's not fair, you know, that all you ever have to do to your hair is brush it. And how you managed to get red hair and those gorgeous black eyelashes, too——'

'Marvellous invention, mascara.' Cassidy fluffed her napkin out and spread it carefully across her turquoise skirt.

'I'll bet you bought that outfit at a discount store,' Heather added bitterly. 'And it looks better than anything in my whole wardrobe.'

'You might feel better about the whole idea if you were eating a civilised meal,' Cassidy pointed out.

Heather shook her head. 'I gained two pounds last week, and at this rate I won't be able to fit into my graduation gown, much less my dress for the spring formal.' She broke off a bit of toast. 'You know half the guys who come to the house any more are more interested in seeing you than the girls.'

The idea made Cassidy a little uneasy. 'Heather, you know I don't encourage anything of the sort.'

'You don't have to. It's that soft look you've got—as if you're always wrapped in a peaceful little cloud, no matter what kind of hell breaks loose around you. It makes men go mad, you know. How did you learn to do that, anyway?'

Cassidy smiled, a little. 'I haven't any idea what you're talking about.'

Footsteps clattered down the stairs, and a sophomore girl in a long nightshirt, her hair wrapped in a towel, burst into the room. 'Cassidy, Melanie borrowed my fuchsia sweater for her date last night and now it's got a stain all down the front of it. I think it looks like *crème de menthe*, and what she was doing with *that* when she's not even supposed to be drinking——' She thrust the offending garment at Cassidy.

Cassidy sighed, inwardly. Just another normal morning at the Alpha Chi sorority house, she thought.

'There,' Heather said triumphantly. 'You're doing it right now! That look of yours——'

Cassidy ignored the interruption, and the sweater. 'Have you asked Melanie what happened, Laura?'

'No—she's still asleep, the lazybones. She was out till after curfew.'

'I know—I let her in.' And I'll be discussing it with her before the day is out, Cassidy thought. 'It was conscientious of her to return the sweater before she went to bed.' She looked steadily at the girl over the rim of her cup.

Laura shifted her weight from one foot to the other. 'Well, actually, I went and got it this morning,' she admitted.

'Oh? I thought we'd all agreed that you girls wouldn't trespass in each other's rooms.' Cassidy pushed her chair back. 'I'm sure you and Melanie can come to an amicable agreement, Laura. Taking care of it yourselves would be much better than if I had to ask the governing council to settle it, don't you think?'

She was almost to the kitchen door when she heard Heather grumble, 'And she was up till the middle of the night. She's got great bones and a terrific figure and to top it off she can party all night and never show the effects. It's just not fair to the rest of us.'

'Maybe some day you'll lose your baby fat, Heather,' Laura said, with devastating frankness. 'Cassidy might have looked just like you ten years ago, when she was your age.'

Cassidy smiled a little, ruefully, and pushed the swinging door aside. Ten years ago, she'd been a slightly pudgy fifteen-year-old, certainly nothing like the worldly-wise Heather. But the air of mature wisdom was one well worth cultivating for a woman in her position, even if it didn't do wonders for her ego when her charges added a few years to her age. And as for that look of—what had Heather called it? Peacefulness—oh, yes, as if she were wrapped in a peaceful little cloud, no matter what happened around her. Well, she had earned that look. And it wasn't an experience she would recommend to her charges, that was for sure...

In the kitchen she checked over the menus for the week and compared notes with the assistant house-mother, who was also the cook. It was an exercise they referred to as synchronising their calendars—with thirty-two young women to keep track of, someone had to be on hand at all times. Thank heaven for a reliable assistant, Cassidy thought as she walked across the car park to her small car. There were moments when she wondered if taking on this second job had been such a brilliant idea after all. In the last four months, since she had moved into the house, it seemed she hadn't had more than fifteen minutes to herself.

But she quickly shrugged off the question. One did what one had to do, she reminded herself. And the result, if the unpleasant reality was faced without bitterness or complaint, was the look of peaceful acceptance that Heather had commented on.

At the first traffic light, she flipped through her appointment book. She'd been promised fifteen minutes this morning with the mayor of one of the outlying suburbs, to discuss his city's current budget crisis. It would probably take the rest of the morning to chase down the details and write the story. And of course there were still the loose ends of yesterday's stories to follow up—the drug bust that had shocked one of the city's best neighbourhoods, the warehouse fire that had crippled a major industry, the progress being made in strike talks at one of the hospitals...

It would be another hectic day, but no more so than most; it was part of being a general-assignment reporter, and Cassidy relished every minute of it. She loved the idea of every day being different, of never quite being able to predict what might happen next.

She wound the car windows down to let the soft breeze in. It was the first really warm day of spring; it had come a little later this year than was usual in Kansas City. It was almost the first of May, and in other years there had been days like this in late March—days when the air was soft with the promise of another summer on the way, another winter survived——

'Bad choice of words,' she told herself briskly—almost automatically—before she'd really stopped to think. But it didn't ache any more, the way it had in previous springs. The warm breeze, the bright sunshine, the scent of new growth no longer brought the crushing weight of dread down against her heart as it used to do. There was sadness, but that was to be expected. All the years of her life there would be sadness when the first warm day of spring came around.

The interview with the mayor went well, once he got over the shock of discovering that the hazel-eyed young redhead across the desk from him really was the reporter who'd just finished the hard-hitting series on how local industries had polluted the Missouri River.

'You're C.R. Adams?' he said several times, sounding almost defenceless. 'But you're so young——'

'And I'm a woman, too,' Cassidy added helpfully. 'Don't feel bad, Mr Mayor; quite a few people make the same mistake. Now, about this tax increase you'll be asking for——'

The mayor shook his head. 'I'm not used to pretty reporters,' he murmured.

But eventually, with persistence, she got her answers. More than that, she got an invitation to lunch at the mayor's club, which she gently turned down. She was always half amused now when someone was taken aback by her age and her presumed inexperience, and her sex. She hadn't always found it funny, but she had quickly discovered that the contrast between her byline and the reality often worked to her advantage, keeping an interview subject just far enough off balance so that she got answers to questions other reporters could not even have asked.

She worked out the first paragraphs of the story in her head as she drove back to the newspaper office, and by the time she reached the sprawling single-storey building—once a supermarket—which now housed the Kansas City *Alternative*, she could almost feel it taking shape in her head.

Still, she stopped for a moment as she got out of the car, looking, as she did whenever she approached the office, at the big block letters that stretched down the entire side of the brick building, spelling out the name. It was the oddest name for a newspaper that she had ever heard of, she had thought the first time she had come here, to apply for a part-time receptionist's job. What sort of newspaper called itself an *Alternative*?

A new one, the editor had explained to her that day. A fair one which wanted to give its readers a choice. An idealistic one which took the editorial position that the older newspapers in the city had joined the establishment and were no longer asking the difficult questions that were necessary for the health of the community.

'Idealism,' she told herself drily. 'We've all got plenty of that, or we'd have given up this mad venture and started manufacturing widgets or weaving baskets or selling houses by now, instead. Something we could make a little money at——'

'Talking to yourself again, Cassidy?' A young reporter brushed past her at the half-wall that set the newsroom apart from the rest of the building. 'Isn't that a symptom of something dreadful? I can't recall what. Brian's been looking for you all morning, and he's acting like a wounded bear.'

'He knows I was on an interview,' Cassidy said, almost to herself. 'He assigned me that story——'

'Well, I wouldn't go barging into his office just at the moment—the big boss is in there.' The young man wiggled his eyebrows meaningfully. 'And when the publisher comes to see the editor you can bet there's something unpleasant in the wind.'

Cassidy sighed and made her way down the long row of battered government-surplus desks to her own olive-green one. She turned on her computer terminal and was halfway through the preliminary draft of her story, making notes on things she still needed to check out, when a sticky little hand clutched at her arm. 'Cassy,' a small shrill voice declared, and a three-year-old girl climbed up into her lap.

The child's mother was only steps behind. 'Oh, for heaven's sake, Theresa,' she called. '*Not* on Cassidy's lap, you're covered with chocolate——'

'She's all right, Chloe.' Cassidy reached for a tissue and wiped off the worst of the mess. 'As long as she's still got more freckles than chocolate spots, I'm not worried.' She settled the child more comfortably, the small compact body fitting neatly against her chest, the sweet-smelling dark hair nestled just under her chin, and closed her eyes tightly for a moment. Sometimes, when she held Theresa, she could almost convince herself that somewhere another precious child was playing, or snuggling down for a nap——

Or throwing a tantrum, she reflected wryly. Fudge would probably have been particularly good at that, all things considered...

She forced her attention back to the young woman beside her desk. 'How was your trip to San Francisco?'

'Great. That reminds me.' Chloe McPherson swung her bulky handbag down on the corner of Cassidy's desk and started to rummage through it. 'It's ridiculous, the number of things a woman has to carry around to keep one small child functioning—— Here.' She pulled out a long, slightly wrinkled envelope and handed it to Cassidy with a flourish. 'Your receipt, ma'am.'

Cassidy opened the envelope just enough to see that it contained the carbon copy of a money order drawn on a San Francisco bank, and leaned down to tuck it safely into the bottom of her handbag. 'You mailed it?' Her voice was a bit muffled.

'From the main post office, precisely as ordered, the morning before I came home.' Chloe looked a bit troubled. 'Cassidy——'

Cassidy gave her a big smile. 'Thanks, Chloe. You're a true friend.'

'And that means that's the end of the subject, right? I wish I understood why you're sending Reid Cavanaugh money. It's not as if he's a charity case or something.'

'A debt is a debt.'

'All right, all right—so you owe him some money. What did you do, anyway—embezzle it?'

'Hardly. I told you—it was a loan.' Her conscience prickled a little, and she thought, It's not really a lie, and Chloe doesn't need the details. It would only encourage more questions.

'Then why go to such lengths to pay it back? A personal cheque would do the same thing.'

'But if he doesn't cash a cheque, the money stays in my account. This way he has no choice about accepting it, at least. Even if he tears up a money order, it's just like destroying hundred-dollar bills——'

Chloe pounced. 'And why would he want to tear it up? Unless *he* doesn't see it as a loan, or a debt!'

Cassidy sighed. 'Oh, for heaven's sake, Chloe—next you'll be thinking I'm paying blackmail money or something.'

Chloe's eyes brightened. 'Are you? Though I can't think what you could be blackmailed for—you're so pure you could compete in the Miss America pageant.'

Cassidy bit her tongue and said, gently, 'Not quite. I think you'd better come back to work soon, Chloe. Six months as a full-time mommy and your nose for news is beginning to fail—it's leading you off course.' She set Theresa off her lap and turned her attention back to the softly glowing computer screen. The child had been happily banging on the keyboard, and the last paragraph of her story had turned into gibberish. She was still trying to fix it fifteen minutes after Chloe and Theresa had gone, but it wasn't the damage to her story that bothered her.

I should never have confided in Chloe, she thought. I forgot that a reporter of Chloe's calibre never quite gets over that insatiable curiosity, that urge to take everything apart just to see what lies at the heart of the thing and makes it all fit together. And I can't exactly blame her for being suspicious; the story I told her was full of holes. But it would have been worse if I'd told her the entire truth.

And I couldn't pass up the opportunity she gave me, Cassidy reminded herself. San Francisco was perfect, and I'm going to have to trust people sometimes; I can't just take off once a month and fly somewhere to handle it myself.

And she could not let down the smokescreen she had so carefully constructed between herself and Reid Cavanaugh. She had no idea if he had tried to trace her in the eleven months since she had sent that first money order from Chicago, but she had no intention of letting him guess that she was still in Kansas City after all. She didn't know what his reaction had been when he received that first envelope, either, but she could guess; he was proud, and having the money thrown back in his face was almost guaranteed to stir him to fury. She had seen him furious, a couple of times—once when she had accused him of paying blood money—and she didn't care to see it again...

'Cassidy!' It was a roar that started in the corner of the newsroom and culminated by vibrating her desk till she thought there had been an earthquake. She jerked upright, looking guiltily around towards the editor's office. She had forgotten that Brian wanted to talk to her.

Hastily she gathered up her notebook and the first computer-printed draft of her story and hurried across to the glass-walled corner office. Brian Erikson was the fairest man she had ever worked for, but she had learned long ago that it didn't pay to keep him waiting.

Today looked as if it would be worse than usual, she thought, pausing in the doorway. He was leaning back in his big chair, feet propped on the corner of his desk. The cigar which was ever-present in the corner of his mouth, and which he almost never lit, was chewed virtually to shreds; the interview with the publisher must have been exceptionally unpleasant, Cassidy concluded.

'Shut the door,' he growled. 'Where have you been all morning?'

She handed the story across the desk without a word. Brian glanced at it and tossed it back. 'I forgot about that,' he said. 'It shouldn't have taken you all morning, anyway.'

'What a gracious apology,' Cassidy murmured sweetly.

'It's a compliment. You're too good a reporter to spend half a day on a piddling story.'

'Why do I feel as if there's a cobra sneaking up behind me?'

Brian removed the cigar from his mouth, put his feet down, and leaned across the desk confidingly. 'I've got a peach of a job for you tonight.'

'Tonight? Brian, you know I've got responsibilities at the sorority house now. I can't just——'

'You've got responsibilities here, too. Which is more important to you?'

Cassidy bit her lip. That wasn't very wise, she told herself. 'The newspaper, of course. But can't someone else handle this? You've got another shift of reporters, you know, and I'm not supposed to have to work nights.'

'What the hell kind of reporter are you if you won't go after a story no matter what time it is, Cassidy?'

'Brian, I need some advance notice when you've got evening assignments for me——'

'I'm giving you notice,' Brian said. 'And you'd have had more notice if you'd been here all morning.'

'That's not——' She stopped abruptly. 'All right; you win. What's the big event?'

'You're going to a cocktail party. Five hundred bucks a head, with the proceeds going to the local shelters for the homeless.'

She stared at him for a long moment. 'Well, isn't that just great? When did you transfer me to the society pages?'

Brian gave her a crooked smile and said, without rancour, 'Keep up the impertinence and I'll put you in charge of persuading the local clergymen to write sermons for the religion column.'

'Do forgive my runaway tongue,' Cassidy murmured. 'The cocktail party sounds like so much fun, Brian.'

'Besides, it's your kind of story. Just think of the poetic contrasts in the situation—it's a benefit for the homeless, while most of the people who will be there tonight have two houses. Three if you count the recreational vehicle or the cabin cruiser——'

'I get the idea. You want a deliciously ironic little piece.'

'Nope. Write it straight. I don't care much about the cocktail party, anyway. I want you to take advantage of all the connections. You're going to be rubbing elbows tonight with the elite of Kansas City, and you never know when one of them might fit right into a story. This series of yours on people who are being squeezed out of the mortgage market, for instance——'

'That's not the same thing as being homeless.' A tiny trickle of dread seemed to slide down Cassidy's throat. 'Where did you say this cocktail party was?'

'Mission Hills; where else?' He scrabbled in the pile on his desk blotter and tossed a slip of paper across to her. 'That's another of those poetic contrasts, Cassidy. It's being hosted by a guy who's made his fortune building condominium developments where even the smallest unit goes for more than a quarter of a million dollars. Do you know how many homeless people you could house for the price of one of his condos on Quality Hill? And I'd hate to think what he spent on his own place—any time somebody builds a house in Mission Hills and modestly calls it a cottage, it must have cost a mint.'

Cassidy wasn't listening any more. She was looking at the slip of paper, at a street address that might as well have been engraved on her heart, for all the chance she stood of ever forgetting it. 'Reid Cavanaugh,' she said quietly.

'You know the name?' Brian looked startled. 'I'm surprised. He's not one of the ones who makes a big show of things—he's not on the mayor's advisory group or the governor's re-election committee or even a museum board, that I know of. In fact, I don't think the guy does much of anything but build condos. I'm surprised he's even giving the party.' Brian's feet went up on the corner of his desk again, and the cigar went back into the corner of his mouth. He moved it around till it was comfortable and said contentedly, 'Maybe you can get an interview with him, Cassidy. It would polish off your new series with a flourish if you can find out what's really going on in the housing industry, from the elusive Mr Cavanaugh's point of view.'

'Brian——'

'And don't give me any garbage about how you can't do it, Cassidy. If anybody can get an interview with Reid Cavanaugh, you can. And tonight may be your best chance.'

Cassidy locked herself in the ladies' room and sat on the corner of the lavatory counter, her chin resting against the heel of her hand. Her temples were aching as if someone had closed a vice across her forehead, and there was a sick emptiness in the pit of her stomach.

'If anybody can get an interview with Reid Cavanaugh, you can.' Well, that was true enough, she thought bitterly. She should have no trouble at all—except that she probably wouldn't be the one who was asking the questions.

'I suppose it was inevitable,' she told herself. 'If you're going to be in the news business in this town, you should expect to run across everybody who is anybody, sooner or later.'

Dumb, she thought. Very dumb, Cassidy Adams, not to consider the possibility.

But she had not. After all, general-assignment reporters for small, struggling newspapers spent their time chasing fire engines and politicians and homicide detectives. They were not invited to the same places as millionaire contractors were. And Reid was not—never had been—the kind of man who made news, or sought to do so. He had always liked his private business to stay private, no matter to what extent he had to go to keep it that way...

'That's interesting,' she muttered. She had never looked at it quite that way before; she had always thought it was only his family pride that had catapulted them both into that mess four years ago——

She jumped as someone began pounding on the door, and slid off the counter to unlock it. 'Sorry,' she muttered as the society editor marched in with a set face.

'What's the matter with you?' the woman demanded.

'Nothing much. I'm just having a massive heart attack.'

The society editor snorted and shut herself in a cubicle. Cassidy resumed her seat on the corner of the counter. It might be fun to psychoanalyse Reid some day, she decided, but just now she'd better be considering her options.

It was certain that Brian would not understand her reluctance to meet Reid Cavanaugh again, unless she went back into his office and poured out the entire truth. And even then, hard-bitten newsman that he was, he would probably not sympathise. He was more likely to rub his hands together in glee and announce that she had a chance to get a once-in-a-lifetime story. No, there was no point in confiding in Brian.

So she would have to work around him, that was all. She would go to the party, she would avoid Reid, and tomorrow she would tell Brian that she hadn't been able to talk to him—or, better yet, that he had refused to be interviewed. It would be stretching the truth, but not

excessively, and she might get by with it; Brian wasn't
likely to call Reid himself and ask why he didn't want
to talk to a reporter.

She groaned a little. Don't kid yourself, she ordered.
Attend a party at that house and avoid Reid? She might
as well try to avoid traffic by walking down the middle
of the road. The Cottage had not been designed to ac-
commodate large crowds, and hiding in a corner would
be an impossible task.

'Dammit,' she said under her breath.

'Are you truly ill, Cassidy?' the society editor asked.
'Or are you just malingering?'

'Neither,' Cassidy said with dignity. 'I'm getting myself
in the right frame of mind to do a story on waste dis-
posal. You've heard of method acting, I'm sure? Well,
this is method reporting.' She stared the society editor
into silence, but as soon as the woman was gone she
leaned her cheek against the cool mirror and thought
fleetingly about a hospital room with a 'No Visitors' sign
on the door. Not even Brian could argue with that excuse,
surely, if they carried her away on a stretcher...

But it would not be a long-term answer, so she went
back to her desk instead and tried to concentrate on
translating the mayor's proposals for a layman's understanding. And she tried not to see the shadow that seemed
to hover just off to the corner of her eye—a very large,
very dark shadow. One that, for the last year, she had
thought was beginning to fade away.

Mission Hills, separated by only a narrow boulevard
from the urban sprawl of Kansas City, might have been
part of another world entirely. Here, in one of the
smallest and wealthiest communities in the nation,
narrow streets wound sinuously through quiet tree-
covered hills, a seemingly random pattern of deceitful

twists and turns. At every curve of the street, another mansion nestled, each more beautiful than the last.

Cassidy had always had trouble driving through the community; whenever she thought she had the pattern figured out she found herself back on the boulevard instead, and she had finally concluded that the people who had drawn the street plan had intended it to be that way to keep the uninitiated at bay. But this time, when she really would have liked to get permanently lost, she had no trouble at all going straight to Mission Drive, to the hillside that sloped away from the street and looked down over the new green grass of the country club golf course. To the cream-coloured brick house that had been almost brand new four years ago, when she had last come down this street.

The Cottage. Reid had told her once that the description had been intended as an insult by the neighbour who had first called it that. 'Why, it isn't anything much at all,' she had said. 'It's only a cottage!'

But it was a fitting name, and it had stuck. The house did look a bit like an old-world cottage, with its low profile and shingle roof and dark-brown shutters and trim. And though it was not at all cramped or dismal or dingy, in comparison with its grand neighbours it certainly did look small. But looks, she had found, were sometimes deceptive.

Cassidy parked her car a long way down the street and took her time, picking her way carefully across prize-winning lawns, the grass already green and thick under her feet. It was another of those contrasts which in other circumstances would have tickled her sense of humour; in Mission Hills people devoted more money every year to nourishing their lawns than most city families spent to feed themselves.

Judging by the number of cars lining the street, the party was already in full swing, but people were still arriving. Cassidy followed a small group up the path, past a trickling fountain and between a low-spreading evergreen and a burning bush whose swelling buds promised luxuriant foliage to come, and held her breath as she stepped across the threshold into the house that—for a brief few weeks almost four years ago—had been her home.

The crowd in the foyer seemed to shift and sway before her eyes. Between bodies, she could catch only a glimpse of the wide staircase leading down to the lower level, and beyond it the formal living-room at the back of the house. But she didn't need to see it, really—that simple glimpse had told her it was still the same blend of soft neutral and pastel colours, forming a subtle frame to what had always been the glory of the house: the views from almost every room across the hillside that sloped down to a winding creek and the country club beyond.

'Your ticket, please?' a soft voice at her elbow said, and Cassidy had the impression that it was not the first time the question had been asked. She handed over the complimentary ticket Brian had given her.

The elegant young woman at the tiny ticket table looked puzzled. 'You're with the Press?' she asked softly.

'I'm C.R. Adams of the *Alternative*,' Cassidy murmured.

'Of course. Natalie will show you around.' A second young woman looked up from the dining-room next door at the sound of her name, and came quickly into the foyer. 'Get Miss Adams a Press kit, won't you, Natalie? And I'm sure she'll want to talk to our director. And of course to Mrs Cavanaugh. Where did she go, do you think?'

Mrs Cavanaugh. It shouldn't have been a surprise; Cassidy certainly had reason to know how smoothly Reid could negotiate his way through the bureaucracy with the least possible publicity. Still, surely she should have heard about it by now if he had a wife—especially a wife who was devoted to causes like sheltering the homeless...

The crowd in the hallway dissolved, momentarily, as one group of people descended the wide, curving stairs and a handful of others started to climb back to the main floor. In that instant, for no reason at all, Cassidy looked up from the young woman at the table and stared across the width of the foyer at the tall man who had just reached the top step. He laid one strong brown hand on the carved newel post, raised the other, which held a sherry glass, to his lips, and stared back at her, his forehead slightly furrowed, as if he was angry——

I shouldn't be surprised at that, she thought.

The clatter of the party faded—or perhaps it was only drowned out by the rush of blood pounding in Cassidy's ears.

Four years—he could have changed so much in that time that she wouldn't have recognised him at all. But he had not. He was still tall and lean and straight, without an excess ounce of flesh. His hair was still that odd mix of black and platinum, and as for the stern set of his jaw——

The front door opened and a stray shaft of late sunlight passed over her shoulder and caught in his hair, turning it entirely to silver.

And then, precisely as if he had consulted his personal catalogue of faces and found her not worth remembering, his brow cleared, and Reid Cavanaugh turned away. A moment later she heard his laugh, strong and clear, ringing out above the noise of the crowd, as if he had not a care in the world.

CHAPTER TWO

It TOOK a full minute after Reid Cavanaugh was out of sight for Cassidy's breathing to return to normal. She didn't know what she had expected him to do. She had not anticipated that he would create a scene, because it wasn't in his nature—but to ignore her altogether, to turn away without a word, as if he felt no curiosity at all about why she had suddenly reappeared——

Well, if that is the way he wants to play it, she told herself firmly, I'm certainly not fool enough to chase after him and explain! I'll simply do the job I was sent to do, and get out of here—and it'll be that much easier if Reid stays out of my way.

She smiled at the young woman who was waiting to escort her. 'I can manage to find my way around, thanks,' she said pleasantly, as she took the slick folder of information. 'And I wouldn't like to take you away from your duties. Who did you say is the director of the organisation?'

She made a note of the name in her minuscule notebook and descended the stairs to the lower level of the house, as far as she could get, for the moment, from the living-room where Reid had gone. She tried to ignore the emptiness in the pit of her stomach. It was never easy to mix at functions like this, to brush up against people she'd never met before and start a conversation that might some day lead to a story. It was like hanging out in a singles bar, she thought drily, except that in the bar one usually had a friend or two to fall back on!

24

The wide staircase ended in a pleasant little sitting area with glass doors that led out on to a secluded patio. A portable bar had been set up at the base of the stairs, and she paused beside it. The bartender looked up enquiringly.

'Do you have water?' Cassidy asked.

The man snorted. 'With this crowd? Do ducks fly? We have tonic water, sparkling water, seltzer water, Perrier water——'

'Just ordinary cold drinking water. In a martini glass, with an olive.'

He looked at her for a long moment and then shook his head and followed her instructions.

'Have you seen Mrs Cavanaugh lately?' It was careless, and she didn't even look at him as she sipped her drink and nodded approvingly.

'Not for an hour or so. I think she's upstairs.'

'Thanks.' She savoured the olive, drained the glass, and set it back on the bar. 'One more, please.'

'For the road?' the bartender muttered. 'At this rate you can drink everybody at the party under the table.'

Cassidy smiled. 'That's the general idea.' She took the glass and wandered out towards the patio, where despite the crisp early evening air a number of people had gathered.

It was no wonder that they were braving the chill, Cassidy thought; the house itself was 'standing room only'. It had never been intended for this sort of crowds; *she* must have invited everyone who lived in Mission Hills...

Within an hour Cassidy had made a number of new acquaintances—that, she thought, should satisfy Brian—but she still hadn't managed to talk to the director of the fund-raising effort. The girl at the ticket table was looking a bit harassed by now, and she scarcely looked up from her ticket stubs as she told Cassidy that she thought the woman was talking to some special patrons in the small sitting-room, just down the hall, first door on the right.

There was a small sinking feeling in Cassidy's heart. So far she had been almost successful in ignoring the house itself, by concentrating on the people and pretending that the familiarity of the wallpaper and the furniture and art was only an eerie coincidence. But to walk down that hallway towards the bedroom wing, and to go into that small sitting-room, which had once been her private retreat...

The director was not in the little sitting-room. Cassidy cast a quick glance around, intending only to make sure the room was empty. But something about the room clutched at her heart. It was still decorated in the soft peach and blue tones she remembered, but now it was no longer coolly charming, waiting patiently to welcome the next guest. There was a difference in the very air; the room had taken on the warmth of constant use, and the personality of its occupant. The cushions on the chintz love-seat were tumbled, and the pale blue chair by the window showed the tiniest signs of wear. On the desk blotter lay a pen and a folded sheaf of stationery half thrust into an envelope, as if the writer had been interrupted in mid-sentence. And beside the blotter stood a small silver-framed photograph.

Cassidy had no intention of prying into the contents of the letter, but the photograph was something else. She had never seen a copy of it before, this picture of a smiling, happy family. She set her half-full martini glass down on the blotter and picked up the frame. Four people looked out at her from their pose behind an unfamiliar fireplace—Reid's parents, sitting together on a brocade sofa; Reid himself, perched on the sofa's arm beside his mother; and Kent—Kent, curled on the carpet at his parents' feet.

It was an old photograph, she thought. In it, Reid's hair was entirely black, but she knew it had been years ago that he'd begun to get those distinguished patches of silver at the temples. And as for Kent—in the photograph his face looked soft and almost baby-round. Surely he hadn't still looked like that on that first warm day of spring four years ago, the day he had lost control of that too-powerful motorcycle on a sharp curve...

But he might have looked like that, she thought, with a wave of sadness. I didn't realise that I'd almost forgotten his face. I thought he looked more like Reid.

That assumption, she told herself, was probably only a bit of self-protection produced by her own mind, at a time when she had still been profoundly shocked by the death of the man she loved. Perhaps it had been just a part of the necessary healing process.

There was a tiny noise behind her, the whisper-soft closing of a door, and she jerked and spun around, still clutching the silver frame between her hands.

'So it *is* you,' Reid Cavanaugh said. 'The sun was in my eyes, and I couldn't be sure.' It was soft, almost as if he were talking to himself. He took two steps into the room and stopped with his hands braced on the back of a chintz-covered chair. A gold signet ring glinted on his finger, and the cuffs of his shirt sleeves, under the grey herring-bone jacket, were crisply white against his tanned skin.

He looks older, she thought. He has changed, after all. I was too far away to really see him, before.

His hair was almost evenly salted with silver, the remaining darkness feathering into the light patches she remembered at his temples, until it was hard to say which colour predominated any more. His face was thinner, as if his skin had drawn more tightly against the bones. And his eyes—there were tiny, fine lines around them, as if he did not always like what he saw.

'So you're not in San Francisco any more,' he said.

'You got my message, I see.'

'Message?' He seemed to turn the word over in his mind, and then shook his head. 'I got your mysterious money order, if that's what you mean.'

'What's mysterious about it? I'd have thought it was fairly obvious. Oh—I see. I'm sorry if you're having trouble explaining it to—anyone.'

'The only one I can't explain it to is myself. A draft for five hundred dollars, made out to me from someone called C. McPherson. Why, Cassidy?'

Cassidy smothered a sigh; she hadn't had a chance to look at her receipt yet, but she supposed it was inevitable that Chloe would have messed up somehow. Putting the wrong name down—of course, it scarcely mattered now, since the whole subterfuge had been intended to keep Reid from discovering where she was. Now Reid knew—and it was beginning to look as if he didn't much care.

She shrugged. 'I don't see the mystery, myself. You obviously knew who it came from—and what it was for.'

'And since you went to all the effort to hide, why are you here now?' he went on, still very softly. 'Was it just bad timing that brought you here in the middle of this mass of people? Not that I think you're uninterested in the problems of the homeless, but I can't imagine——'

She shifted her feet restlessly. 'That I'd be important enough to make the guest list for this party—is that it?'

'That hadn't occurred to me at all,' he said levelly. 'I just think you'd be down in the streets handing out blankets—not here drinking martinis and discussing homelessness on the theoretical level.'

'I thought the same of you, Reid. This kind of thing isn't your style.'

He turned his hands palms-up for a moment. 'It's not my party.'

'I heard,' she said, a little stiffly.

'My mother wanted to do what she could for the cause, and you must admit *she's* not the sort to be handing out blankets——'

'Your mother?' It was almost breathless. 'I thought——' She stopped, abruptly.

'That I was married again?'

She swallowed hard. He had always been perceptive—so quick sometimes that she thought he was capable of reading her mind. She tried to squash the thought.

'Is there any reason I shouldn't be? The divorce was perfectly above-board, I assure you. But you knew that already, didn't you?'

'I got the papers, of course——'

'How long have you been married, Cassidy?'

'Me?' The shocked monosyllable slipped out so quickly that she had no time to consider whether it was wise.

He crooked an eyebrow. 'You've changed your name,' he said softly. 'C. McPherson——'

She shook her head, and then wished that she hadn't. There was no need to explain to him, after all.

'An alias, then?'

He didn't need to make it sound as if she was trying to avoid the FBI, she thought irritably. 'C. McPherson is my friend Chloe,' she admitted finally. 'I was never in San Francisco.'

He thought it over, and then went straight to the heart of the matter. 'Or in Minneapolis, either, I suppose,' he murmured. 'Or Atlanta. Or—was it Yankton, South Dakota? I'm afraid I've forgotten.'

Obviously it hadn't mattered to him where she might be. That, she thought, puts you firmly in your place, Cassidy.

'So you've been here in Kansas City all the time.'

'Most of the time, yes.' She set the picture frame carefully back on the desk. When she turned around again he was giving her a careful head-to-foot survey. She was uncomfortably aware of his gaze; he was assessing her as if she were a particularly troublesome blueprint.

It didn't seem to bother him that he'd been caught at it, though. He simply finished inspecting her, from red hair smoothly drawn into a smooth knot at the back of her neck, over the neat turquoise dress, to slender ankles and toes impatiently tapping inside pumps chosen more for comfort than for style. 'You're even thinner than you used to be,' he said.

'I'm not pregnant now,' she said crossly. 'Of course I'm thinner!' Then, as he continued to look at her impassively, Cassidy bit her tongue and wished that she hadn't reminded him. 'My hair is longer, too,' she added. 'That doesn't mean anything, either.'

'It wouldn't take much—your hair, I mean.'

'I know,' she said drily. 'From the back, I used to look like a boy.' He had told her that once—it had been almost the first thing he'd ever said to her, as a matter of fact. Did he remember that? Was it her imagination, or was there the slightest twinkle in his eyes?

'You still haven't told me why you're here tonight— at the Cottage,' he reminded. 'My first thought was that you needed money, but——'

'Not at all,' she said stiffly. There was certainly no reason not to tell him the truth, she reflected. 'It's my job—I'm a reporter for the *Alternative*.'

Was it surprise that flashed for an instant in his eyes? 'That's a long way from being a middle-school teacher of English,' he mused.

She shrugged. 'I tried it. Couldn't stand the little brats. Then this came along, and I liked it.' She picked up her martini glass again and drained it at a gulp. 'Actually, I'd like to interview you some time, Reid. Get your views on the housing situation in Kansas City—that sort of thing.'

He didn't give her an immediate and implacable refusal, which was what she had expected. Instead, he said slowly, 'I'll think it over, but——'

'Please do. You know where to reach me.' She fidgeted with her glass for a moment then set it firmly back on the desk blotter. There was really nothing more to say.

'I shall.' There was a note of patient politeness in his voice; he seemed to be waiting for her to leave.

Just go, Cassidy, she told herself. Don't prolong this any more. Don't make him tell you to leave!

She did not hurry away from the Cottage. Until she was out of sight, down the street and in her car, she walked slowly, like a lady. It was one of the hardest things she had ever done.

The sorority house was quiet. Curfew had come and gone, and tonight no one had pushed the limits. In fact, Melanie, the young woman who had been so late the night before, had been waiting in the small office reserved for the house-mother when Cassidy had come in. That had been some help, Cassidy thought as she got ready for bed. It was bad enough trying to enforce rules on young women who in other circumstances would be completely independent. But when the rules were essentially unenforceable, as the curfew was—— What did one do with a young woman who came in late, after all?

Refuse to let her go out ever again? Ask the girls on the governing council to throw her out of the sorority altogether?

She turned the lights off and drew the curtains back from her bedroom window and curled up on the window-seat. Melanie's reaction worried her; it wasn't normal for a girl of that age to accept a reprimand in almost total silence——

'Don't pretend,' she ordered herself. 'The thing that's bothering you is how much like you Melanie is—head-strong, certain that she's right. Convinced that the rules which apply to ordinary people don't quite fit for her.'

And, like you, she added silently, Melanie may find out some day that the rules do apply—and that down deep, no matter how hard she tries to convince herself otherwise, she believes in them after all...

That lesson had been harsh in the learning for Cassidy. It had all looked so clear, that autumn more than four years earlier, when she had met Kent Cavanaugh in the coffee shop where she worked near the campus, and a few weeks later moved in with him. What could be so wrong about it? she had asked herself—on the rare occasions when she had allowed herself to think about it at all. They were in love. They would be married as soon as Kent graduated and was no longer so dependent on his family. And in the meantime, they shouldn't have to suffer just because Kent's mother didn't approve of his choice. She would come around, some day soon. She would have to accept Cassidy, or risk losing Kent. So Cassidy cheerfully sent him off to spend Christmas with his mother in the East, knowing that next year nothing could take him away from her. And the following March, on the first warm day, Kent took his motorcycle out for the glorious first long ride of spring, and he missed a sharp curve and went over an embankment...

It was at the door of the hospital's intensive care unit where Cassidy learnt the harsh fact that a girlfriend, no matter how intimate, was not family and therefore was not allowed to see the patient. She waited outside, too terrified to be angry, too numb to question—and only after Kent's life had ebbed away and she'd watched from a distance as his mother left the hospital, leaning on the arm of her only remaining son, did it occur to her to wonder if it had been the hospital's rules, or Jenna Cavanaugh's request, that had kept her away from Kent's side.

She told herself that it didn't matter; in his coma, Kent could not have known whether or not she was there with him. But she suffered from the guilt, none the less, and for a while she thought that her life, like Kent's, had ended in that grinding crash.

The funeral was private, and so Cassidy had only the comfort of a memorial service in the university chapel. It was probably just as well that she hadn't been at the funeral; as it was, she nearly fainted in the middle of the memorial service, and only the action of a couple of alert friends in promptly getting her out into the cold wind—the promise of spring that had taken Kent's life had been just a flirtatious fancy after all—kept her from embarrassing herself completely.

She didn't know then that she was pregnant. She thought it was only the shock of losing Kent that made her feel so ill for the next few weeks. But by the middle of May, she faced the truth, and she began to look dispassionately at a future that held little promise for her or for the child she carried. With her part-time job at the coffee shop, she could keep herself going; with the help of loans and grants she could finish her remaining two years of college and get her teaching certificate. But with the baby's birth everything would change. She could not earn enough to support them both; she could not manage a baby and a job and college as well. And unless she could finish college there would never be a hope of anything more than grinding poverty for both of them.

Kent's child deserved better than that.

There was no one for her to turn to for help. Her own parents were so long dead that she scarcely remembered them, and as for the aunt who had raised her—well, Cassidy had no trouble predicting what Aunt Sandra would have to say to an unmarried, pregnant niece.

She even considered writing to Jenna Cavanaugh, but she shuddered away from the idea. A woman who could refuse to allow her son's love even to attend his funeral would have little sympathy for her plight now.

So Cassidy made her decision. Harsh and wrenching though it was, it was the only course she could take.

That was the way things stood the night that Reid Cavanaugh came into the coffee shop and took a booth in her section. She recognised him from the brief glimpses at the hospital and at the memorial service; there weren't many men who had his height, his elegance of dress or the silver patches showing sharply against the dark hair at his temples. Or that aura of certainty that came, she thought, from being obeyed far too often for his own good...

It was only coincidence which had brought him there, she told herself. After all, he lived in Kansas City; it was nothing so unusual for him to stop at a coffee shop. So she set a glass of water on the paper place-mat in front of him, handed him a menu, and began to tell him about the evening's special, just as she would with any other customer.

'You're Cassidy Adams,' he said.

Her white and startled face must have confirmed it, for he didn't wait for an answer. 'When do you get a coffee break?'

'I don't.'

'Then when does your shift end?'

'Why does it matter to you, Mr Cavanaugh?'

'So you know who I am.' It was almost silky. 'I'll say one thing for Kent. You may look like a boy from behind——'

'Only on my good days,' Cassidy said tartly.

He grinned at that, but the shadow of cynicism stayed in his eyes. 'But you're no idiot. I'll bet you even know already what I came here to talk about.'

Her heart was fluttering so fast that she couldn't quite get her breath. 'Sorry to disappoint you, but I can't think what you'd have to say to me.'

'Don't play dumb.' He sipped his water slowly, and watched her over the rim of the glass. 'I want to know what you're going to do about Kent's baby. Bring me the special—whatever it is—and a pot of coffee. There's no hurry. I'll be here till closing, or until you leave—whichever comes first.'

There was a shadow on the lawn of the sorority house. A dog? A trick of the moonlight, perhaps? Or a prowler, stalking the house? One of the sororities up the street had reported a peeping Tom, a couple of weeks ago.

Cassidy watched the shadow for long minutes, until she was certain that no human being could have stayed still for so long.

Then, with a sigh, she turned away from the window. Don't be a fool, she told herself. You know perfectly well there's nothing out there. But you'd rather face the bogeyman in the dark than your own memories, tonight...

*   *   *

Reid had been as good as his word that night; it had been almost midnight when her work was done, and he had still been sitting patiently in the booth, drinking coffee, idly turning the pages of the morning's newspaper. She had had a couple of hours to think it over, and so when she came back to the booth for the last time she was considerably calmer. Perhaps Kent's family had a right to know what she had decided. In any case, it seemed, it was no longer her choice whether to tell them; the man in that booth was a force to be reckoned with.

'I've clocked out,' she said. 'I'm finished for the night.'

He pushed the newspaper aside. 'Would you prefer to talk here, or somewhere else?'

She must have looked a little surprised.

'You're thinking that there isn't all that much to talk about,' he speculated. 'Is that it? You make your demands and I meekly agree to them—is that what you expect to happen?' He waved a hand at the opposite side of the booth. 'Sit down.'

She did, but only to avoid drawing the attention of the night waitress and the few other customers in the coffee shop.

'You might as well tell me what you want, Cassidy.'

She thought bitterly, You'll never believe it—but why not tell you? 'A good home for my baby,' she said. 'That's all. So I'm giving him up for adoption, and you can just run along and not worry about it any more.' She started to slide out of the booth.

He said, impassively, 'That makes things much easier.'

Cassidy stopped. 'What on earth do you mean?'

He didn't answer. 'When is the baby due?'

'Why do you care?' But she couldn't hold out against that cool stare. 'The middle of December.'

'December,' he repeated thoughtfully. 'Have you talked to an agency yet?'

'Yes, as a matter of fact. They told me there are hundreds of people who are desperate for babies—people who will give him love, and security and a good education——'

'And every toy and game and thing he fancies,' he agreed. 'Some of those people are so desperate to have a child that they smother the babies they adopt, you know. They ruin them, turn them into selfish, spoiled brats by giving them more material possessions than any child should have——'

'It isn't only adopted children that happens to.'

'True enough,' he said. 'Take Kent, for instance——'

'Don't talk to me about Kent!' It was sharp. She closed her eyes, tightly, and said quietly, 'I've considered that. I'll have to take my chances, won't I?'

'But the idea bothers you, doesn't it?' He was silent for a long moment. 'And they'll pay your expenses, of course.'

'Are you suggesting that's wrong? Look, Mr Cavanaugh, if I could afford to be noble I'd never have considered giving my baby up in the first place!'

'And you'll never have to see him again, or be reminded——'

She bit her tongue hard. 'That is a filthy thing to say,' she said. 'Do you think I came to this decision easily? I don't see that I've got a choice—it doesn't seem to me to be very loving to condemn a child to the kind of life I could give him.'

'You could have come to me.'

'You?' It was shrill and unbelieving. 'When you and your mother wouldn't even allow me into the intensive care unit to see Kent, you expect that I would come begging you for help so I could keep his baby?'

'Not exactly.'

'Then what—exactly—do you have in mind?'

'First——' He leaned across the table. 'Do you want a cup of coffee or something?'

'No. Caffeine seems to make the morning sickness worse.'

'Milk, then.' He looked around for the night waitress and sent her off, over Cassidy's protests.

When the tall glass of milk arrived, she stared at it for a long moment, and pushed it aside with a contemptuous hand. It almost tipped over. 'You were saying?'

'First, you have to understand that I had no idea Kent had a little cupcake sitting outside his hospital room.'

'Right,' Cassidy said drily. 'Just where did you think I was, anyway—out celebrating?'

'Dammit, don't you understand? I never knew you existed. It wasn't till they carried you out of the memorial service that it occurred to me that Kent's love-life had been awfully quiet lately, and when I started asking around——'

'Do you expect me to believe that? Your mother was furious at the idea that he wanted to marry me——'

The cynical glint in his eyes had sharpened. 'If she was, she certainly didn't tell me.'

'You don't believe me, do you?' Cassidy said quietly. 'That Kent was going to marry me.'

He shrugged. 'What difference does it make now?'

She looked down at her hands, nails cut short, skin reddened by the strong disinfectants she used every day, fingers bare. Kent had said he intended to buy her a diamond, as soon as his next allowance came . . . 'None, I suppose,' she whispered.

He toyed with his coffee-cup, and when he finally looked up he said, 'I want the baby, Cassidy.'

'You?' Her voice was heavy with disbelief.

'Think about it. You want a safe, secure home for him—an education, the love of a family. So do I—but I want it to be his own family.'

'What about your mother?'

'I haven't discussed it with her. It's none of my mother's business.' It was uncompromising.

Cassidy's eyebrows raised. It had been her impression, from what Kent had said, that Jenna Cavanaugh considered everything to be her business.

'I promise you the child will be cherished, and not spoiled or over-indulged. I swear to you that he will grow up to be a decent human being——'

She found her voice again. 'What——?'

'And that he will know about the loving sacrifice that his mother made when she gave him up——'

'You want me to just hand him over to you?'

He traced a pattern on the paper place-mat with the handle of his spoon. 'You're going to hand him over to someone,' he reminded quietly. 'Why shouldn't he have his proper heritage, Cassidy? His real name?'

She put her elbows on the table and buried her face in her hands. A faint smell of bleach clung to her fingers, from the cloths she had used tonight to wipe the tables. It seemed to mingle with the scent of Reid Cavanaugh's cologne, and the combination stung her nose with the harsh contrast they represented for her baby. Reid's words echoed through her mind.

'You're going to hand him over to someone. Why shouldn't he have his proper heritage. His real name?'

She might not exactly like Reid Cavanaugh, but could she blame him for what he wanted to do? This was his brother's child. And what about the baby? An agency would be very careful to place him in a good home, but might he be better off with his blood uncle?

It isn't like Aunt Sandra, she told herself. Aunt Sandra never wanted you—but Reid Cavanaugh wants this child.

This way, a little voice at the back of her brain reminded, you will know what happens to him. You'll know where he is, and who he is. The agencies won't allow that . . .

That's selfish, she thought. I have to decide what's best for the baby.

If it were my brother's child, she thought, and he were dead, what would I want to happen? What if I had been this child, and some day I was told that my mother had had a choice, and she had chosen to send me away from all my family, forever?

She didn't look up. 'Very well,' she whispered. 'I agree.'

'I think that's a very wise decision.' But he didn't sound in the least triumphant. 'You can give your notice tomorrow. I don't like the idea of you working at this kind of job.'

The proprietorial tone set the hair at the back of her neck on end. 'And what business is it of yours? What do you expect me to live on?'

'I'm planning to pay your expenses, of course.' He stared at her, his eyes narrowed. 'Don't be foolish. It can't be good for the baby when you're on your feet for ten hours at a time.'

Cassidy's eyes dropped. He was right, after all.

He took her silence for consent. 'Then there's just one problem left,' he said. 'That's the adoption routine itself. You said you've already contacted an agency?'

'I haven't signed anything. It's far too early.'

'That's good. But I'm sure you understand that even private adoption has its hazards in a case like this. I'll be a single parent, you see, and that still isn't the most popular arrangement with some judges.'

'I'm sure you'll work it out.'

He didn't pause. 'Even more important, as I'm sure the people at the agency have already told you, you have certain parental rights that can't be terminated till after the baby is born. If you were to change your mind in the meantime——'

She shook her head. She was extraordinarily tired, all of a sudden, and she didn't even have the strength to ask just where he expected her to run to with a newborn!

'I'd like some sort of guarantee that you can't just walk out on our agreement, Cassidy.'

She shrugged. 'Whatever you think you need,' she mumbled. 'Though I assure you it isn't necessary.'

He looked at her for a long moment. 'I'll make the arrangements, then.'

Something in his tone warned her, and she looked up, suddenly alert again. 'Just what do you have in mind?'

'It's very simple, really. My attorney worked it out. It avoids the entire problem of adoption, by creating a more regular family unit.'

She stared at him for a long time, silently.

Finally he sighed and said, 'I mean a marriage of convenience, Cassidy. As your husband, in the eyes of the legal system I'll be the father of your child——' He saw the shock in her face, and went on hastily, 'For heaven's sake, girl, I'm not suggesting that we should share a bed! I don't intend that we even live under the same roof. I just want to ensure that this child ends up in my custody, and that it's done as smoothly as possible, and with as little damage to him——' He paused for a moment, and added, softly, 'It would mean that he wouldn't be illegitimate, you know.'

'What does that matter, any more?' she said bitterly. 'These days——'

'But I think it does matter to you. You were very anxious to convince me that Kent wanted to marry you.'

She stared at her hands, knuckles white, clenched on the edge of the table.

'You've already agreed to all the difficult things, Cassidy,' that relentless voice went on. 'Why stop at this? It's only a formality, for the baby's sake. A few months——'

'No,' she said. 'No.'

But he didn't seem to hear her. 'It's for the best; you'll see. Drink your milk,' he ordered. 'And then I'll take you home. You need all the sleep you can get, just now.'

CHAPTER THREE

IN THE end, Cassidy married Reid, for the baby's sake, and—if she was completely honest about it—for her own peace of mind as well. She had known all along, of course, in some detached corner of her brain, how very difficult it was going to be to give up her child completely, to sever all ties, to not even know his name or whether he was healthy and well-adjusted. She had put that knowledge aside, however, and told herself that she would get used to the idea as the months passed, and that when the moment of truth came she would be all right, because she was acting in the best interests of the child.

But when she was offered a chance for something else——

It wasn't much, of course. Reid wanted his brother's child, and perhaps he felt a small obligation to the mother of that child. But he had been very honest about what he was offering her, and what he would not give. He would send her a photograph and a summary of the child's progress each year, along with a cheque for ten thousand dollars, in return for her continued co-operation...

That was when she said something about blood money and the way in which babies were bought and sold on the black market. It was the first hint she had ever had that Reid Cavanaugh was capable of fury. The angry glitter in his eyes, the stern set of his jaw, the taut white line of his mouth, shocked her; he was totally unlike

Kent, who exploded and swore and threw things. Reid's controlled anger was, she thought, more frightening.

Then, abruptly, the emotion was gone. Reid reached for her hand and said, very reasonably, 'I understand that you're scared, Cassidy, and worried about whether you're doing the right thing. But I'm *not* buying the baby! We'd made our agreement before the money ever came into it.' He saw the uncertain trembling of her lower lip, and brushed it with his thumb, adding gently, 'It's not all that much, you know—money doesn't go as far as it used to. And lord knows you're going to need it.'

That was true enough. So she bit her tongue and let him set up a special bank account and make the first deposit on the day the dry words of a judge made them husband and wife. Or perhaps it was more fitting to refer to the arrangement as Reid had, that night at the coffee shop—they were now 'a more regular family unit'.

She swore to herself that she would take his help only as long as she must, that she would regard it as a loan, and that some day she would pay every penny back, because to do anything else was to put a price-tag on her baby.

She did it, too—as far as she was able. Last May, she had finally finished at the university, and on the first day of June, when the annual cheque was deposited, she closed the account. She took every remaining cent of Reid Cavanaugh's money to Chicago with her when she went to a news reporters' convention, and she bought the first of that series of money orders. And every month thereafter she would send a little more, until she had paid back the part of his money she had spent...

The moon was high now, in the wee hours of the morning, and the shadow out on the lawn of the sorority house stayed solidly in place.

It was funny, Cassidy thought, with a yawn, that he hadn't pursued the question of why she had tried to hide.

Something creaked above her head, as the old house settled itself for the night. Cassidy's head drooped against a needlepoint pillow, and moonlight caught in her eyelashes and cast long shadows across the hollow of her cheek.

Perhaps, she thought, as she slid towards a sleep that could no longer be denied, he hadn't had to ask. Perhaps he already understood. Or perhaps he honestly didn't care...

The morning's issue of the *Alternative* was lying on her desk the next day when she got to work, and on the lower half of the front page was the first article in her series on Kansas City's housing problems. It explained, succinctly and sympathetically, the problems faced by young people who wanted to buy property but couldn't afford to get into the market because even starter homes were priced above their reach.

The people she had interviewed had been frank and open and very quotable, and the finished story flowed easily. Good job, Cassidy, she told herself as she finished reading it. The next few articles were already done and waiting for space; she thought, privately, that they were not quite as good as this first one, but then mortgage brokers and estate agents were sometimes not as easy to talk to as the average citizen was. And that left her with only the final few stories to do, to tie up the loose ends. What a block-buster it would be, she thought, if she could produce Reid Cavanaugh as her final story...

You should have stayed in bed a bit longer this morning, she told herself. You're still dreaming!

She kept a wary eye on Brian's office while she opened her mail and cleared up the work left over from yesterday, but his door remained firmly closed. Cassidy had half expected that he would call her in, curious to know what the cocktail party had been like last night——

Damn, she thought. I never managed to talk to the head of that fund-raising committee after all; it just went out of my head after my chat with Reid. And I've got to write the story today.

She had just reached the woman by telephone and settled back in her chair to ask a few questions when a stir at the receptionist's desk caught her attention. Cassidy's desk was too far away from the front of the building for her to hear the words that were exchanged, but it didn't need much interpretation to guess their meaning; a moment later the receptionist stood up and pointed towards Cassidy, and a tall man with silvery hair turned and walked across the big room straight towards her.

A quizzical question from the woman at the other end of the telephone line interrupted the silence that had suddenly fallen. Cassidy gathered her wits with an effort, bent her head studiously over her notebook and went on asking questions. But from the corner of her eye she watched as Reid approached, his step unhurried but firm. His dark grey suit fitted to perfection; he unbuttoned the jacket as he arrived beside her desk, and sat down in the old metal chair which stood invitingly empty across from her. He propped one elbow on the arm of the chair and looked around as if he was fascinated by the bustle of the newspaper office.

There were no more questions to ask; Cassidy thought she had probably already roused hopes in the chairman of a much bigger story than the cocktail party deserved. Nevertheless, she ended her telephone interview with a bit of reluctance. 'I'll be with you in a moment,' she said, without looking up.

'No hurry,' Reid said equably.

She made meaningless marks on paper for a couple of minutes and then pushed the notebook aside. 'What can I do for you?' Instantly, she regretted phrasing it quite that way; it implied all sorts of possibilities.

Reid hadn't seemed to notice. He gave her a cheerful smile and said, gently, 'Good morning, Cassidy.'

It would have been very rude not to respond to that friendly greeting, impossible not to smile back at him. He had always been good at exerting his will, that way, she thought; he had certainly done it to her countless times before. Cassidy supposed this was the method he would have used to discipline Fudge, too... She called a quick halt to that line of thought; there was no sense in allowing herself to think about that.

'Good morning, Reid,' she said briskly. 'And now that the formalities are over—do I dare hope that you've decided to let me interview you?'

'No,' he said. His gaze roamed over the long rows of desks with interest.

Cassidy decided that she didn't have to play cat-and-mouse. 'Well, if you'd like to subscribe, the circulation manager has a desk by the front door. And if you'd like to place an ad, that's the far corner.' She waved a hand towards the appropriate office, then pulled the keyboard of her computer terminal closer and began to edit the story she'd left on the screen.

'I'm not saying no to the interview, necessarily; it's just that I haven't decided yet,' Reid said. 'So I decided to come in and look the place over.'

'That's not generally——' She bit her tongue. It might not be standard procedure for a news source, but then Reid wasn't the usual interview subject, either. She didn't for a minute believe that he would actually give her that story, but, as long as he hadn't actually said a firm no, she supposed that she couldn't just throw him out. 'I suppose you'd like the grand tour?'

'If you've time.' He rose so quickly that Cassidy thought, a bit nastily, that he might have springs in the soles of his shoes.

'I can't think of anything that's more important today,' she muttered, and wasn't surprised when he smiled a little at that. But he didn't say anything, and as she showed him around Cassidy's suspicions began to fade; he was obviously interested.

The building had once housed a supermarket, she told him, and he nodded as if he remembered it well. Now rows of desks filled the single gigantic room that took up most of the front half of the building. Here and there a nook had been walled off, mostly with temporary, head-high partitions, but most of the staff worked in the open.

'It must make it difficult to concentrate,' he said.

'One learns. At least we have computers that are fairly quiet—if we were trying to work with typewriters clacking, we'd all be deaf. And the owners promise that by next year we'll all have private offices.' Cassidy shrugged. 'Of course, they've been saying that for three years now, so——'

'The newspaper isn't doing well?'

She shot a wary look up at him, but it was an innocent enough question. 'It's doing very well. Starting up a daily newspaper requires a phenomenal amount of capital in any circumstances, but when you you go head-to-head with established ones——' She shook her head. 'Besides, a nice office might make a reporter happy—and then again it might not—but it certainly wouldn't improve the product for the reader. Right now, we'd rather put the cash into keeping more reporters working so we have a better newspaper.'

'You're a very effective salesman,' Reid mused. 'In fact, it sounds like you're a part-owner.'

'All the employees are shareholders. Very minor shareholders, but still——' She shrugged. 'The dividends may one day buy my morning coffee.'

'You've been with the newspaper since it started, then?'

'Almost. I started part time while I was still in college, and when I graduated there was an opening for a reporter so I moved up.' She opened a door in the wall that closed off the back half of the building and gestured at the dark, unfinished room. 'We're supposed to get our own press, too. But, since offset printing plants cost hundreds of thousands of dollars, we're not holding our breath.'

'Perhaps at the same time you all get offices?' Reid murmured.

She smiled. 'Probably. In the meantime, we do as much of the production work here as we can, and then a job printer in one of the suburbs does the actual printing.' They were back in the newsroom now, and she took a deep breath and knocked on Brian's door. 'I'll take you in to meet the editor.'

Brian Erikson was quick to take a hint, she'd grant him that. He looked like a thunder-cloud for a moment when she stepped inside his office, but, as soon as his eyes focused on the man behind her, he blinked once and then turned an approving smile on Cassidy.

Before he could get any big ideas, she introduced Reid and added hastily, with a meaningful glare, 'Mr Cavanaugh is considering letting me interview him, Brian——'

'Good, good,' Brian said. 'It'll be a great story, Mr Cavanaugh; we need more visionary leaders in this city, and we're always happy to help them get their views across to the public.'

Cassidy thought, That's quite enough flattery, Brian! She had seen the tell-tale twitch at the corner of Reid's mouth, and she knew—though she didn't quite understand why she was so certain—that he was dying to laugh. Funny, she thought; I never realised that I'd noticed that sort of thing about him.

Another reporter knocked on the door, and she breathed a sigh of relief. 'We'll get out of your way, Brian, and finish our tour.'

Brian offered his hand. 'Very good to meet you, sir. You're on expense account, Cassidy. Take Mr Cavanaugh to lunch.'

She wanted to groan.

'That sounded like an order,' Reid observed.

'Don't feel obliged, Reid. Brian's a bit——'

'I wouldn't want to get you in trouble with your boss. Do you need a jacket or anything?' He fished her handbag out from under her desk and gave it to her, and before she quite knew what she was doing she was outside the front door of the newspaper office, being tucked solicitiously into the front seat of his Lincoln. She couldn't help noticing that it was a brand-new one—dark blue this time, with leather upholstery so soft it was like butter.

She sank into the softness and sighed. 'If you're really so anxious that I not get in trouble with Brian, you'll give me that interview.'

'I haven't said I wouldn't, have I?'

'You haven't said you would, either,' she muttered.

He smiled. 'Shall we go to Felicity's for lunch?'

She sat up. 'Wait a minute—*Alternative* expense accounts aren't all that good.'

'Don't worry—we'll put this one on my bill, and save you from Brian's wrath.'

'When you don't give me the story after all.'

'What a pessimist you are, Cassidy.' He started to whistle as he negotiated traffic.

On the road a motorcycle sped past them, far faster than the legal limit, and cut in ahead of the Lincoln so sharply that Cassidy gasped and threw her hands up over her face.

Reid hit the brakes, and a moment later when everything was clear again he glanced at her. 'It still bothers you, then.'

She stared straight ahead. 'Not as much as it used to,' she said woodenly. 'Just when people drive like fools.'

After a long moment he said, 'It wasn't the first motorcycle he'd wrecked, you know. He was just luckier, before.'

She didn't answer, and a moment later he started to talk again about the *Alternative*, and for the rest of the drive they discussed the market share the newspaper had managed to carve out against its older, more established competition.

Felicity's had developed a reputation as one of the top ten restaurants in Kansas City, and there were often waiting lists for tables. Cassidy was not surprised, however, when the *maitre d'* took them straight to a secluded corner. The only thing she wasn't certain about was whether Reid had planned this and made a reservation, or if he got this kind of treatment all the time. She wouldn't be surprised if it was the latter.

He murmured an order to the waiter while she was absorbed in her menu, and a couple of minutes later she found herself staring at a martini that had silently materialised in front of her. Reid sipped his iced coffee and said, 'The seafood salad is about the best thing they do here.'

She nodded. 'That's fine.' She handed the menu over and looked around. 'They've redecorated,' she said, determined not to let him think that she was completely out of her league here.

He seemed unimpressed. 'It seems to be necessary to stir things up once a year to keep the clientele happy. Personally, I liked it better before.'

'You don't care much for change, do you? I noticed the whole Cottage is just the same——' She stopped, abruptly, and then said with determination, 'I hope you'll read my story in this morning's paper.'

'Oh, I already have.' It was bland. 'Did you choose your self-effacing byline with me in mind? Just in case I picked up the *Alternative* some day?'

She had, of course, but she wasn't about to admit it.

'It was probably wise of you. There could be any number of people in Kansas City named C.R. Adams, but Cassidy is considerably less common. In fact,' he mused, 'you've grown a great deal more distinctive in the last few——'

'What did you think of the story,' she interrupted.

'I found it very interesting.'

She let the silence drag out. You shouldn't be disappointed, she told herself, but she still found herself saying, 'Is that all? Interesting?'

'Should there be more?' The waiter brought their seafood salads. Reid picked up his fork and went on, 'I'm reserving judgement till I see the rest of the series. How long will it go on?'

'There will be a half-dozen stories scattered over the next several weeks. Perhaps you'd better subscribe after all.'

'Perhaps I should,' he murmured. 'I'd hate to miss anything you had to say. Do you get so personally involved in all your stories? This one seemed to have a particularly sympathetic slant, as if you were one of the people most affected by the problem.'

'And you'd rather I'd confined myself to cold, hard facts?'

'I didn't say that.'

'It's not a cold-hard-facts sort of story, you know. And I do feel sympathy—I haven't run up against the difficulty myself, exactly, but——'

'But only because you haven't tried to buy a house?'

'What difference does it make whether I have or not?'

He shrugged. 'None at all, I suppose.'

'How do you feel about the problem, anyway?' she challenged. 'Or haven't you given any thought to the people who'd like to own a house, but can't afford to buy the sort of thing you build?'

His eyes sparkled. 'Off the record? I wouldn't care to be quoted——'

Cassidy sighed. 'Never mind.' She stabbed a scallop, half wishing it were him.

'Where do you live now, Cassidy? You can't be making all that much money at the *Alternative*, and with the money orders you're buying every month it can't leave much——'

'I don't recall inviting you to worry about my finances, Reid.' It was both quiet and determined.

'Who said I was worried?' His voice was equally quiet. 'I'm just curious.'

And that, Cassidy told herself, puts you firmly in your place. Did you expect that he was going to beg you to take his money?

'You haven't finished your martini,' Reid said. 'Is there something wrong with it?'

She was just annoyed enough to be truthful. 'I never drink the things.'

His eyebrows went up almost to his hairline. 'But last night——'

'It's a trick Brian taught me long ago. Carrying a cocktail glass around helps a reporter to mingle in a crowd like that, and putting water in it instead of alcohol keeps the reporter on her toes instead of under the table. Normally I just drink orange juice and let people assume it's got vodka in it, but last night the olives looked good.' She toyed with the tiny shrimp that topped her seafood salad.

He was silent for so long that she began to worry about it. 'I should have known you hadn't turned into a lush,' he said finally.

'Thanks for the compliment.' She sounded disgruntled.

He smiled and waved the waiter over. 'What would you rather have instead?'

'Nothing, really; if he'll just take this away, I'll be happy. Some coffee later, perhaps.'

The martini disappeared. Reid offered her a hot roll from the basket at his elbow and said, 'My mother announced this morning that she would like to meet you, by the way.'

Cassidy almost choked on a shrimp. 'Why on earth——?'

But she didn't have to ask, really. Jenna Cavanaugh's reasons would be apparent to anyone with the slightest bit of intuition. It was a natural enough reaction, Cassidy thought, for Mrs Cavanaugh to want to assess the threat that Cassidy represented, to see whether she was likely to cause trouble yet again.

'It would help me out of a difficulty,' Reid admitted.

And the translation for that, Cassidy thought, is that once she sees me she'll stop nagging him...

'Forget I asked,' she said crisply. 'But if it's such a big problem for you, why did you bother to tell her I was there last night?'

'What makes you certain that I did? She's quite capable of finding out who was at her party. And as for the half-hour or so that we were alone in her sitting-room——'

'Oh, she knows about that too? Then she probably thinks I'm trying to blackmail you.'

'I'm sure the thought has occurred to her.' It didn't seem to bother him. 'Dinner some evening this week, perhaps?'

'I'm sorry, ' Cassidy said with cool politeness. 'I have very little free time just now. But do tell her how sorry I am that I won't be able to see her while she's here.'

'That covers a lot of territory, you know,' he said mildly. 'She isn't just visiting me for a few days—or didn't you realise that she's living at the Cottage now?'

It made sense; why else would the woman have got so involved in local causes that she was throwing cocktail parties to aid them? Cassidy could have kicked herself for being so dense.

'This weekend, perhaps?'

'Do I have to spell it out for you in blood, Reid?' she asked sweetly. 'I defy you to give me one good reason why I would want to have dinner with your mother.'

He smiled at her, very gently, and countered, 'Give me one good reason why I'd let you interview me, Cassidy. I don't need publicity, you know. My work speaks for itself—if I build a solid condominium complex, it doesn't need a public relations campaign to sell it. And if it falls down under its own weight, no public relations campaign could save it, either. So——'

'Who's blackmailing whom?' she said bitterly.

He gave her an innocent, wide-eyed smile. 'What about Sunday, seven o'clock? Surely the *Alternative*'s editor lets you have a day off sometimes, or does he lock you in the bottom drawer of his desk between assignments?' He snapped his fingers. 'That explains it. That way, you don't need a place to live at all, so of course you have money to burn——'

Cassidy decided this had gone far enough. 'What I do with my money is my concern, Reid!'

He said sombrely, 'But I'm not supposed to give any thought to what you're doing with mine?'

She bit her tongue, hard.

'Why are you sending that money back, Cassidy?'

Her hazel eyes were wide and earnest. 'I should think you, of all people, would understand that. *Because* it's your money, Reid—don't you see? I certainly didn't do anything to earn it.'

There was a long silence, and then he said, a little stiffly, 'The doctors all said the miscarriage wasn't your fault.'

She looked at him levelly. 'But you've never quite believed them, have you?' She folded her napkin with hands that wouldn't stop trembling, and laid it aside.

'How would you know what I believe?' he asked quietly. 'You didn't even wait for me to get there before you walked out of the Cottage and disappeared——'

'And saved us both a great deal of embarrassment,' Cassidy said softly. 'It was over; nothing was going to bring the baby back. Now, I really need to get back to work.'

'You haven't had your coffee——'

'I also haven't got a promise of an interview, which is what Brian was hoping for when he encouraged this. And I'm not in the mood to play games about it, Reid. If you decide you'd like to talk to me, fine. If not—

well, don't start hanging around the *Alternative* office just for fun.'

He drove her back to the newspaper office in a silence that would have been deafening, if the pounding in her head hadn't been even louder. She told Brian that the chances of getting a story from Reid Cavanaugh were approximately equal to the odds of her becoming the next Pope, and walked out of his office before he could demand an explanation.

She buried herself in her work, and managed to subdue all the old memories and get her work done, but it all washed back over her at the end of the afternoon when she finally reached the quiet serenity of her own two little rooms at the sorority house and her mind was free to roam. The sheer nerve of the man, expecting that she would meekly be coerced into allowing his mother to cross-examine her *now*——

It had never been in the plans for her to meet his mother, or at least he had never mentioned such a possibility to her. So far as she knew, he hadn't even broken the news to Jenna Cavanaugh that she was going to be a grandmother. Cassidy hadn't let it concern her much, though she had wondered, from time to time, whether he planned to wait until the baby was born. Privately, she hoped that was exactly what he intended to do. She had no idea whether Jenna was likely to be sentimental because something of her lost son had survived after all, or irate at the idea of Cassidy's child being part of her family, but at least Cassidy herself would be gone before the family firestorm began...

Not that she had worried about it. To tell the truth, she hadn't done much thinking at all in the early part of that hot summer; it had hurt too much to think. She'd missed her job; it would at least have given her some reason to care what time it was. Most of the time she simply stayed, alone, in the tiny efficiency apartment she had moved to after Kent had died.

Reid came to see her at least twice a week. Sometimes he took her out for a meal, sometimes he insisted that she come for a walk with him. But—as he had promised her—he made no other demands.

Then one afternoon he dropped in unexpectedly with a bag of groceries, and when he opened her refrigerator to put the food away he discovered that there was nothing inside but a quart of milk and an untouched head of lettuce.

'Did you have lunch out today?' he asked mildly.

'No,' she said without thinking, from in front of the television set.

'Did you eat at all?'

She eyed him warily and told the truth. 'Nothing tastes good, Reid.'

And that was the second time she had ever seen Reid Cavanaugh become furious, and she quickly learned that the first time had been hardly worth mentioning in comparison.

He stalked off to the far corner of the apartment, tugged a suitcase out from under the folding couch-bed, and started throwing clothes into it at random.

That got her attention. 'What in the hell do you think you're doing, Cavanaugh?'

'Taking you, and everything you own, out to the Cottage where I'm going to make damn sure you eat. I don't give a whoop in hell about you, Cassidy, but you're damn well going to wait till after the middle of December to starve yourself to death!' He finished filling the suitcase in icy silence, and when he turned to take her arm she pulled away.

'You can't just drag me out of here screaming.'

'Want to bet?' he said grimly. 'In this neighbourhood, I could probably get by with a great deal more than that!'

He was right, so she didn't bother to scream. She went downstairs with dignity, and got in his car—it had been a cream-coloured Lincoln, then—and he took her out to Mission Hills. The first time she ever saw the Cottage was when she and her suitcase were ignominiously dumped in the foyer while Reid went off to seek out the housekeeper. Mrs Miller was a plump, homely little woman who clucked over Cassidy and then bustled off to the kitchen and began to cook a continual procession of tiny, delicious dishes.

Cassidy didn't know if it was the food, Mrs Miller's gentle bullying, or the atmosphere of the Cottage—so different from the tiny apartment—but within a week she was feeling better. She actually laughed at the squirrels one morning as they played on the deck rail outside the breakfast-room. Reid put his newspaper down and watched her, and after that they had breakfast outside every day, and she patiently bribed the squirrels with titbits until one of them would boldly come and sit on the arm of her chair and take peanuts from her hand.

It felt strange even to say it, but it was a happy summer, despite the tragedy that had preceded it and the pain that she knew was yet to come. She didn't let herself think about the future; December was a long way off. In the meantime, her cheeks were becoming positively plump; her skin had a sort of inner glow, and her hair was growing from the severe boyish cut into an Orphan-Annie mop of red-gold curls. The day she turned twenty-one, Reid took her to a play she had long wanted to see, and that night she felt the first fluttery movements of life. She was teary-eyed with happiness, and at the same time frightened, as if this were a moment snatched from time, an instant too precious to last...

And, of course, it had not lasted. Ten days later, while Reid was in Washington, DC for a conference on new standards in the housing industry, she woke in the middle of the night with a feeling of malaise, and before the day was out her pregnancy had ended itself. A spontaneous abortion, the doctors told her. Obscene words, she thought. There was no obvious cause for it, but of course the shock she had been through and the fact that she had been so drastically underweight hadn't helped...

In a way, losing the baby was an even harsher blow than Kent's death had been, and she lay quiet and pale and wordless in her hospital bed.

It took them hours to find Reid, but he called Cassidy's hospital room as soon as he knew what had happened, and told her that he would be on the first flight back to Kansas City in the morning.

'Don't,' she said. 'Please don't. There's nothing you can do. I'd much rather you stay and finish your business.'

There was a long silence on the telephone, and then he said, quietly, 'We'll talk about it when I get home, then. Take care of yourself, Cassidy.'

That was all. It had a dreadfully final ring to it, but at least, she thought, he hadn't actually told her to leave. She didn't think she could have borne it if he had, and she was determined that he would not do so.

Mrs Miller came the next morning to take her back to the Cottage, and within a couple of hours Cassidy had quietly gathered up her things and stolen away, leaving a note propped up on the bureau in the room that would have been the baby's nursery. She thought it was probably the first place he would go.

And she had gone back out into the world alone, and once more summoned up the will-power to pick up the scattered pieces of her life.

CHAPTER FOUR

DAYS crept by without another glimpse of Reid, and gradually Cassidy relaxed. She would never have bet any money on the possibility of getting an interview with him, but she had thought—and foolishly—that he might make a nuisance of himself, wanting answers to all sorts of inconvenient questions. Actually, now that it was all over, she was a bit annoyed at herself for having been so much on edge over meeting him again, when Reid obviously hadn't considered it important enough to upset himself about.

Why had she bothered with all the nonsense—the childish, underhand, cloak-and-dagger games? How ridiculous it all looked now—the hours she had spent plotting out ways to deliver that money to him, month after month, so that he couldn't trace her down and force it back in her face, only to find out that he apparently didn't care where she was or what she did...

Just thinking about it made her feel a little dizzy from embarrassment. She could feel the heat from her toes all the way to her hairline.

'Who do you think you are, anyway?' she asked herself. 'James Bond? Well, I've got news for you, my girl—the intelligence forces of the world are not waiting in line for you to get tired of journalism as a career!'

And, since she had already devoted a great deal more time to the matter than was justified, she put down her paperback biography of Dolley Madison—she hadn't been comprehending much of it, anyway—and went up to the third floor of the sorority house to see how the girls were coming along with their decorating job for the formal dance they were giving the following weekend.

The house had once been an elegant family home, complete with a third-floor ballroom that stretched the length of the house under a high sloping ceiling and peeped out to the front and back through small dormer windows. Every year the sorority's governing council considered remodelling it into bedrooms and baths and increasing the number of girls who could live in the house. Every year the same council voted it down, for a combination of practical and sentimental reasons. The practical concerns included the difficulty and expense of providing a reliable heating system and water supply. But Cassidy had got the impression that the sentimental reasons were more important to most of the girls. The main one seemed to be the dance that the Alpha Chi house hosted every spring, near the end of the term. It was always the last formal event before the pressure of final exams week began, and the last big social gathering before the campus emptied for the summer break.

She climbed the twisting stairs and called, from the top step, 'Is it safe for me to come up here, or shall I retreat till the giggles stop?'

Since no one shrieked a warning, she went on. A half-dozen girls were sprawled on the polished oak floor; others were perched on ladders and window-seats. Heather looked up from a yoga-like pose and said, 'Hi, Mom.'

The name was a fairly new development; Heather had taken to calling her that in the last week, as if she wanted to emphasise the age difference between them. Cassidy was getting very good at biting her tongue and smiling about it. 'I hope you appreciate the effort it took to get my arthritic old body up those stairs,' she murmured.

Heather grinned. 'Have a diet soda. All the preservatives might help.'

Cassidy decided that she had lost that round. She reached for the can Heather held out. 'Are you going to be finished with everything in time for the dance? You won't have much time to work during the week——'

'Certainly. We're only taking a short break.' Heather pointed imperiously to a first year in a lavender leotard who was lying on her stomach on the floor. 'Make yourself useful,' she ordered. 'Go bring up another six-pack of the life-sustaining fluids. Nefertiti commands!'

The girl groaned, but she got to her feet and clattered down the stairs.

'Nefertiti?' Cassidy asked mildly. 'Where did she get into the act? I thought this was going to be a soft, romantic little dance—"On the Wings of Love", didn't you say?'

'Oh, we've just been planning our next Hallowe'en party. Don't you think an ancient Egyptian theme would be great? We can't agree if the decorations should be the Pharaoh's court or Tutankhamen's tomb, but the costumes would be a snap.'

Cassidy popped the top of the can of soft drink and sank easily into a cross-legged pose on the floor. 'I can't wait to hear about them,' she said, with resignation.

'Think of all the possibilities. Mummies, of course, and sphinxes and all kinds of animals and birds. I can think of a couple of girls from one of the other houses who are already pyramid-shaped; it's a natural. And as for the Alphas—we can all drape ourselves in gold lamé and black wigs, and not even you could fuss about how much make-up we put on.' Heather smiled triumphantly.

Cassidy shuddered. 'Let's leave that discussion till autumn, all right?' She tipped her head back and looked up; the sloping ceiling was rapidly vanishing under sheets of silver tissue, artistically draped and stapled in place. 'It's starting to look like a sultan's tent in here,' she said warily. 'You wouldn't dare—would you?'

Heather chuckled. 'No, it's just clouds. It's supposed to look as if you're inside them—seeing the silver lining, you know. We got stuck, though, because nobody can reach high enough to put up the last row of tissue sheets.' She glared at the high-peaked ceiling. 'This is our tallest ladder, and we barely got it up here with the turns in the stairway.'

The first year clattered up the stairs again and dropped the six-pack of pop with a bang that threatened to explode all the cans. 'I've got it,' she said excitedly. 'I mean, I've got him—he was just there at the front door. The answer to our problem. Isn't he a tall one?' She flung out her arms in a stagy gesture; the leotard strained across her chest.

Cassidy's back was towards the stairs. She hid a smile at the expressions on the faces of a couple of the girls who hadn't bothered with their usual high standards of dress and make-up today. Then she turned to see which of the young men who hung around the sorority house had been honoured with this unusual view of the sisterhood; his eyes were probably popping out, she thought, and the first year was likely to hear about this violation of privacy for weeks to come——

The man standing at the top of the stairs did not seem moved by the display. His gaze swept over the assembly of youthful beauty with uninterest and came to rest on Cassidy, who decided abruptly that she was going to have a few things to say to the girl herself. Sunday afternoons were sacred, and a woman shouldn't have to worry about dressing up before she left her room. If she wanted to wear faded old jeans and a sweater that in other circumstances might have been considered a little too tight, it was no one's business but her own——

And what was Reid Cavanaugh doing here, anyway? What had inspired him to appear at the sorority's front door? Well, she'd bet on one thing—he hadn't been selling magazines!

The groans and shrieks from her sorority sisters were already informing the first year that she had made a serious mistake. She drew herself up straight and said firmly, 'But he doesn't *count*, you know. He's not really a *man*——'

Cassidy thought there was the merest sparkle of amusement in Reid's eyes, and that tell-tale muscle at the corner of his mouth twitched.

'—he only came to see Cassidy,' the girl went on. 'And I thought he could help us with the high stuff——'

'I'm afraid his labour union won't let him touch a hammer,' Cassidy said. She rose from her cross-legged pose, feeling suddenly stiff and rather awkward.

'He came to see Cassidy, hmm?' Heather purred. 'And just where have you been hiding this one, Mom?'

'I don't belong to the union,' Reid countered.

'That's what I mean—the union that works for you would be very unhappy if you started driving nails yourself.'

'Have you been talking to some of my employees, Cassidy?' It was a mere murmur, and he was already climbing the ladder as he spoke. 'All right—what's the assignment here?'

Heather started handing up sheets of silver tissue. 'Just drape the stuff across the peak of the roof and stick a staple in the corners,' she said. 'If you do too good a job, we'll never get it back down.'

Reid tacked the first sheet up. 'You disappoint me— I thought I could show off all my handyman's skills.'

Cassidy debated whether to stay or leave; on one hand, there was no necessity to stand around and watch while Reid put on some sort of macho act—and what was he trying to prove, anyway? That he wasn't an antique, a mere relic of manhood, as the first year had implied? He'd done that already, she thought—the girls were looking at him worshipfully.

But, if she left, wouldn't it appear that she was running away? She compromised and said, from the foot of the ladder, 'Whenever you're finished, Reid, I'll be in my sitting-room. I'm sure one of the girls will show you the way.'

Then she regretted drawing his attention, for she had to walk the entire length of the ballroom away from him, and she didn't hear a single staple being driven until she had ducked safely out of sight in the stairway. The jeans she was wearing, she thought fretfully, really had been through the clothes drier once too often. They were tight and soft and revealing...

That was exactly why she gritted her teeth and didn't change her clothes. She was not going to admit that she had even noticed his appraising look, much less that it had made her uncomfortable!

It was nearly an hour before a laughing delegation of girls delivered him to her sitting-room. Cassidy put her biography aside—her bookmark had moved on a few pages, but her understanding of Dolley's life had not—and said, 'Do come in, Reid. I'm flattered that you remembered me at all. Or was I jumping to conclusions when I assumed that you came because you wanted to talk to me?'

The sarcasm seemed to glance off him. 'Oh, we don't need to talk at all, Cassidy, if you'd rather concentrate on looking admiringly at me.'

Cassidy stared at him for a long moment. 'The girls have not been good for you,' she said dispassionately.

He flexed his arms. He was wearing a knitted short-sleeved shirt and no jacket, and the muscles rippled under the tanned skin. 'You can say that again. Hanging seventeen plywood stars while balancing on the top step of the ladder was the last straw. If they're going to shanghai a man into doing that kind of work, they could at least invest in some proper tools.' He looked hope-fully around the room, and spotted the tiny kitchenette tucked into a corner. 'I don't suppose you could produce a cup of coffee?'

She jumped up, glad to have something to do with her hands, and started to look for the coffee-pot. 'They didn't even offer you a diet cola?'

He wrinkled his nose. 'I hate the stuff. I'd rather get my caffeine the old-fashioned way. Sorry about that wisecrack I made the other night, by the way——'

'Which one?' She bit her tongue, but it was too late.

'About your getting thinner. You haven't.'

She wasn't quite sure how to take that, until she realised that his gaze was focused on the pattern knitted into the front of her sweater.

'At least, not everywhere,' he added.

'Thank you—I think,' Cassidy said with icy polite-ness. 'However, I assume that isn't what you came to talk to me about.' She located the coffee-pot, on the top shelf of the cabinet above the tiny bar sink. She glanced over her shoulder at Reid, who seemed to have turned his attention to an inspection of the room, so she stretched as far as she could to reach the pot. It escaped her fingertips by a hair, and she started looking for something that would extend her reach.

'Obviously you don't use the kitchen much,' he said, 'or you'd store things where you can get to them.' He came up behind her, almost silently, and reached for the coffee-pot, setting it down right in front of her. For an instant, she was confined in a tiny space between the sink and his body, and his arms were almost around her. There was nowhere she could go, no way to slip away from him——

'Of course, you never were much of a cook,' he reflected, and moved back to his chair.

The tingle in her spine gradually died away. She filled the pot and started it brewing, and said, with a shrug, 'Why cook? It's much easier to have my meals with the girls, and it's part of my job, anyway.'

'I don't quite understand, you know. Why are you doing this?'

She shrugged. 'They pay me a bit, and I've got my room and board. It makes things much easier.'

'And since you don't have to rent an apartment, it gives you cash to buy money orders,' he mused.

She nodded. 'I think it will take about six more years, at this rate.'

'And until then you won't even have a place of your own again?' He shook his head. 'Cassidy——'

'Don't feel sorry for me, Reid—I don't need sympathy. And this is certainly a better neighbourhood than I could afford to live in on my own.' But the fact that he had asked the question made her uneasy; she glanced at the coffee-pot, which seemed to be taking its own sweet time. Why, she asked herself, didn't I just use instant so he could be on his way faster? 'Some day I'll write a book about my experiences as a house-mother—I've already got the title. *Room, But Never Bored*.

He did not seem amused. 'I didn't quite expect this,' he said, looking around the tiny sitting-room. 'When you wouldn't tell me where you lived, I thought you had a resident boyfriend.'

'Why? Because I did once before?' There was a challenge in her voice; she almost instantly regretted the sharp tone. It was, after all, a normal conclusion to draw; she had lived with Kent—why not someone else? She said, more softly, 'Kent was special.'

There was a long silence. 'It wouldn't be a crime, you know,' Reid said. His voice was surprisingly gentle. 'It's been a long time, and no one expects you to mourn forever.'

She shook her head. 'It's not that, really. Oh, I still miss him, and I wish things could have been different. But I wouldn't say I'm still mourning. I just haven't found another man I could care about that way, and I——'

'And you're certain you never will? When on earth do you have time to look?'

She gave him a quiet, level stare. 'I just know.'

'This is not a normal life for a twenty-five-year-old woman, Cassidy——'

'Shush, please.' She gave him a brilliant smile. 'A lot of the girls don't know my age, and I'd hate to disillusion them by letting them know I'm really not old enough to be their mother.' She found a couple of cups in the cabinet. 'I'm not sure if I have sugar—I know there's no cream——'

'I drink it black, remember?' He crossed the room to stand beside her, leaning against the counter. 'You might as well have closed yourself up in a convent as do this.'

'Oh, come on, Reid! That's not a fair comparison and you know it.'

'What's unfair about it? If you have to be here every minute that you're not at the newspaper——'

'Is it your business? I pay my debts, Reid—how I do it really isn't your affair.'

'It wasn't a loan, you know.'

'Well, I saw it that way. So I'm paying it back.'

The tiny muscle at the corner of his mouth tightened. 'For six more years,' he said.

She nodded. 'More or less.'

'And in the meantime you're closing off every other avenue in your life until you've freed yourself of that obligation, is that it? That's crazy, Cassidy—and sick as well. Nobody's expecting that you'll forget about losing Kent and the baby. It wouldn't be natural if you did. But you have to go on living—— '

'Thank you for the highly motivational lecture,' Cassidy said. 'But I went to church this morning, and I really don't need another sermon——'

'You've honestly convinced yourself you don't have feelings any more, haven't you? Repaying that loan isn't a moral issue with you—not really. It's an excuse—an excuse not to rejoin the real world. Heaven forbid you might meet a man you cared about—or one you wanted to go to bed with.'

She frowned a little. 'Aren't you being redundant?'

'No—it isn't always the same thing, and the fact that you don't know that proves my case. You're so afraid of being unfaithful to Kent——'

'I am not!'

'—that you've dug this little hole for yourself and pulled the entrance in after you, so you don't have to face life any more. When was the last time you were kissed, Cassidy Adams?'

'That's really not——'

'Are you afraid?' he asked softly. He took the spoons out of her hand and put them down beside the coffee-pot, and turned her to face him. 'That doesn't sound like the image you're trying to make me believe in.'

Though only the tips of his fingers rested on her shoulders, Cassidy felt as if the weight of the world were holding her there, keeping her from moving. And even if she recovered from her paralysis, there was no place for her to go. The tiny kitchenette was all angles and corners, and she was caught in one of them.

Her heart began to race. Don't be a fool, she told herself. You're certainly not in any danger; one scream and you'll have thirty-two girls in here defending your honour—and giggling behind your back, of course, but that's not the point just now——

The first brush of his mouth against hers was cool, almost clinical, and she relaxed a little. Whatever he was trying to prove, it wasn't going to take long to disillusion him, so why make a fuss about it? To do that would only let him believe that he was right, that she *was* afraid. Far better to co-operate and then let him see how un-moved she was...

So she let her hands slip slowly up his arms until her fingers locked at the back of his neck, and she fluttered her eyelashes at him and murmured, 'Is that the best you can do? What a shame—I usually enjoy being kissed.'

His eyes lit with warmth as if a candle had been ignited in the grey depths. 'And do you enjoy having your bluff called?' he murmured. His fingertips slid from her shoulders to her throat and came to rest against her carotid arteries. For an instant, she thought he was going to choke her. But he was merely searching for the pulse-points just under her jaw, and as soon as he felt the hasty, tell-tale heartbeat he smiled. 'And it's easy to do, too. You must remember that next time.'

'There's a difference between annoyance and excitement——'

But there was no opportunity for further argument. She gritted her teeth and braced herself, expecting that this time he would be fierce and demanding and perhaps even harsh, to prove his point——

But he was none of those. His kiss was warm, soft, persuasive. He caressed her lips, the corners of her mouth, her eyes, her temples—and when she began to protest he took advantage of that as well, his tongue darting softly against her teeth until she couldn't stand it any more, and the longing to taste him began to undermine common sense and whispered in a dark corner of her brain that he was right, it *had* been a very long time since she had been so thoroughly kissed...

Sanity returned with an uncomfortable roar, and she broke away from him and turned to fill their coffee-cups, heedless of the fact that the coffee-pot had not quite finished brewing. 'Satisfied?' she asked. 'Of course I'm not afraid of you. I'm just unimpressed by this habit you have of taking over other people's lives and telling them what to do.' She glared up at him for a long moment and pushed his cup towards him.

'Of course I'm satisfied,' Reid murmured. 'I made my point. Or do you always ignore coffee splashing all over the kitchen because you forgot to put the pot back on the warming tray?'

The coffee-maker was still blithely pumping hot water through the beans, unaware that there was nothing to catch the finished brew. Just then a few drops of boiling liquid hit her hand and she swore and held her fingers under the cold-water tap. Reid hadn't moved, and so she was pressed almost against him again to reach the tiny sink.

She tried to recover her poise. 'Just why did you come here to talk to me today? It wasn't to deliver that lecture, I'm sure——'

'True enough.' He hadn't moved. 'I didn't realise how crazy you'd become till I got here.'

'That is quite——'

'I came to tell you I'd let you do the interview after all.'

Cassidy's eyes narrowed. There has to be a catch, she thought. He just doesn't do this sort of thing, and I can't for the life of me see why he'd change his mind now. 'No deals,' she warned. 'I'm still not having dinner with your mother—I don't believe in special treatment.' It was a masterpiece of sarcasm.

He didn't seem to hear. 'But now that I've had a chance to look at it from your point of view, I think perhaps I should talk to the other reporter first, before I make any decision. It would only be fair, don't you think?'

Cassidy blinked. 'What other reporter?' she managed.

'Do you think you're the only one who'd like to talk to me?' He shook his head sorrowfully. 'Cassidy, I never thought you had an ego problem. And since you don't want special treatment——'

'What other reporter?' It was louder this time.

'You know her, I believe—the name is McPherson. She's with the *Alternative*, too.' He took a long drink of his coffee and set the cup aside. 'You should work on that coffee, Cassidy. It's terrible. I'll show myself out.' He stopped at the door of her sitting-room, and added, 'And don't worry about it. I'll be in touch when I've decided what to do.'

He wasn't bluffing; when Cassidy finally reached Chloe, at home late that night, the woman was candid. 'Thanks, Cassidy,' she said. 'Being a mommy was fine for a few months, but, as you pointed out, I was stagnating. So I talked to Brian, and he's got a place for me on the city beat starting on Monday. I'll try not to trample on your territory—but you know how it is.'

'What about Theresa?' Cassidy asked hollowly.

'Oh, she was much happier in day care than she's been with a crazy mother,' Chloe said blithely. 'I'm so anxious to get back to work—Cassidy, I've got so many ideas rushing through my head that I'll never get them all chased down.'

Cassidy didn't ask whether the story about Reid Cavanaugh was in that category. She just crossed her fingers hopefully and didn't breathe his name at all; she suspected that any mention of him just now would make Chloe even more interested than she already was.

So instead she told Chloe that they had missed her expertise at the newspaper and they'd all be glad to have her back.

He doesn't know what he's getting into if he talks to Chloe, she thought as she tossed restlessly against her pillows that night. And good enough for him, too! she concluded crossly. He deserves all the discomfort he's got coming to him. 'When was the last time you were kissed?' indeed! Any man who could pull off that stunt——

But it wasn't that kiss which floated through her dreams that night. Instead, it was a long-ago caress, the first time he had ever kissed her...

It had been a perfect July night, and the air that drifted through her bedroom windows was the pleasant temperature of a warm bathtub. It caressed her skin like the soft touch of lotion, and it should have put her to sleep within minutes. But the day had been too full of events to let go of easily, and so she lay in the dark and went over it, minute by minute. The sheaf of flowers that had come, with a birthday card, from Reid. The special little dinner that the housekeeper had put together, followed by a candle-topped cake that was almost solid cream cheese—Mrs Miller had good reason to know how much Cassidy had been craving that sort of thing, lately. The tickets to the newest play, which had just finished its run on Broadway. Yes, it had been an almost perfect day.

Cassidy pushed the sheet back and padded across the room to pluck a daisy from the crystal vase of summer flowers, to hold it close to her cheek while she went to sleep. In fact, she thought, it would have been a perfect day altogether if the play had been followed by something rich, sticky, and chocolate.

Just that quickly did the cravings come—out of nowhere, it seemed. She sighed and told herself to think of something else and go to sleep. But the hunger didn't pass, and after a while she put on her robe and went to the kitchen to see if there might be something there which would satisfy her.

Reid was in the family-room. The stereo was playing softly, and a magazine lay open on his knee. The instant he saw her, he was on his feet, concern in his eyes.

'It's nothing,' she said. 'Just a raid on the kitchen, to see if Mrs Miller might have left something lying around.'

'You're hungry?' He looked astonished.

'Not really hungry—but if I don't have a bite of something chocolate I may turn into a werewolf before dawn.'

He followed her into the kitchen. 'What kind of thing do you want? Rocky road ice cream? Chocolate cream pie? Candy bars——?'

Cassidy took her head out of the refrigerator. 'Fudge,' she breathed, wide-eyed. 'The kind that has whole walnuts pressed down on top——'

'It's almost midnight,' Reid said doubtfully.

'Some help you are.' Cassidy found a package of mint chocolate morsels and helped herself to a handful. She ate them one by one, eyeing him all the time. 'First you want me to eat, and now that I find something that sounds good, you——'

He groaned. 'Fudge. Any suggestions as to where——?'

'I'm only kidding, Reid. I'll last through the night.' She turned at the kitchen door and added thoughtfully, 'Of course, if Mrs Miller were still up, she'd make sure I got what I wanted.' She laughed merrily at his expression, and went back to bed in a much better frame of mind.

She'd been sweetly asleep for an hour or so when a knock on her bedroom door roused her. It was probably a mere tap, but in the silence of the house it sounded like an entire army battalion crashing into her room.

She sat up and turned her bedside light on, and tugged her nightshirt down over her knees as Reid opened the door. 'Madam requested fudge,' he said woodenly, and set a crystal plate down on the blanket beside her.

Her eyes went round. 'Reid, you darling!' The plate was lined with fudge, each piece a full inch thick and topped with a half-walnut, pressed down into the chocolate. She picked one up and popped it into her mouth. It was wonderful—rich and sweet and creamy and——

'This is still warm,' she accused indistinctly.

'It'll cool. You wanted fudge, now eat the damned fudge.' He sat down on the edge of her bed as if he was planning to make sure she finished the whole plate.

She looked at him sternly. 'Did you get Mrs Miller out of bed——?' A sudden flicker of movement startled her, and she clutched at her stomach.

'What's the matter?' Reid reached for her.

'He moved!'

He looked at her for a long moment. 'The baby kicked you?'

'Well, it was more like a fish flapping around—but yes, I suppose he kicked.'

Reid grinned. 'He likes fudge, hmm? Maybe we should just call him that.'

Cassidy giggled, and then, with the lightning shift of mood that came so often these days, her eyes filled with tears. It will pass, she told herself. It's only your hormones running wild. She popped another piece of fudge into her mouth.

When she looked up at Reid a moment later, the laughter had died out of his eyes, and he was looking at her almost as if she were a stranger. When he leaned towards her, she didn't even murmur, and when his lips gently—so very gently—brushed against hers, she kissed him back, willingly. It was a soft and tender gesture, the sharing of a precious moment that came only once in a lifetime—and it soothed her battered heart that he was there...

Reid pulled back first. 'Cassidy,' he said, quietly, and there was a note in his voice that was almost fear.

It made her ache, a little, and she tried to cover it with humour. 'I suppose we'll have to lock up every bit of chocolate in the house by the time he starts to crawl,' she said, and even as the rash words spilled out she was horrified at herself. For long before the baby learned to crawl she would have left the Cottage; if this child was a chocolate fiend, the only way she would know was if Reid told her, in those annual reports he had promised. She had proved herself a fool, once more. 'He likes fudge, hmm? Maybe we should just call him that,' Reid had said, and her tired subconscious mind had leaped a chasm no human being could cross...

He rubbed at his eyes. For a single moment that seemed to stretch into infinity she cringed from the fear that he would feel it necessary to explain to her that he had been talking about only the next few months of her pregnancy, and nothing beyond that at all. He would be very gentle, she knew, and that would make it even worse——

'I—forgot,' she whispered. 'I didn't mean—anything.'

He sighed, then, as if in relief. 'Goodnight, Cassidy.'

'Reid——' It was only a whisper, and he turned at the door. 'Thank you for the candy.'

He smiled a little, though it didn't reach his eyes, and added, under his breath, 'Good night, Fudge.'

Then she was suddenly, achingly, alone. She had cried herself to sleep...

For a moment, when she woke, she thought it was July and this was the Cottage, and the nightmare was still to come. Instead, the breeze flowing in through the window held a spring chill, and the room wasn't the quiet guest suite at the Cottage, but her own bedroom at the sorority house, with its mismatched furniture and squeaky floors.

But one thing was the same, on this night nearly four years later. Her pillow was damp with tears for Fudge, and for herself.

CHAPTER FIVE

CASSIDY argued with herself through the rituals of getting ready for work, and by the time she went down for breakfast she had concluded that there was no need for her to become involved. Reid deserved whatever discomfort he got, and it was not as if she was arranging it deliberately. All Cassidy had to do was stay out of it, and let the inevitable happen.

But as she crossed the edge of the campus to her car in the cool brilliance of the spring morning, Cassidy found that, no matter how true it was, she couldn't leave it at that. He didn't know what he was getting into, she rationalised. It wouldn't be fair not to warn him——

'So you're going to offer to hold his hand,' she jeered at herself. 'That's the most incredibly foolish thing you've ever done, you know. He's not a naïve little boy!'

But she stopped at his office, anyway, on her way to work, gambling that his old habits hadn't changed and that she would find him there despite the early hour. She had never visited the headquarters of his company before, but she knew where it was, in one of the new office towers not far from Country Club Plaza. The setting was one of the most impressive in the city. Still, she was not prepared for the office itself, an entire floor of glass and steel and cool, muted colours, with the main display of art being the glorious, ever-changing view of the Plaza from the huge windows.

Reid's secretary admitted that he was in, but seemed doubtful that he could spare a moment for a reporter.

'I'll ask, of course,' she said. 'In the meantime, you might like to look at some of the brochures over there.'

'I think he'll have time for me,' Cassidy told her, and turned her attention to a quite astounding collection of sales pamphlets concerning Cavanaugh condominium complexes.

When the secretary returned, she looked more than a little surprised. 'He'll see you right now.'

His readiness to see her confirmed Cassidy's suspicions, and it should have pleased her to be proved right—but it did not.

Reid's office was on the outside corner of the building, and wide windows on two sides gave a glorious view of Country Club Plaza, its Spanish-mission-styled buildings marching in stately rows up the hillside, each tiled roof catching the light and throwing it back in a slightly different shade of red or gold. It would be an ever-changing panorama, Cassidy thought, and wondered how he ever managed to take his eyes off it and get to work. But it was obvious that he did; on the other two walls, which were panelled in light birch, several huge framed drawings were hanging. She managed a quick glance at the one nearest her. It was an architectural perspective of a condo complex. She didn't recognise the name, neatly lettered in the lower left hand corner; this, she thought, must be an up-and-coming project.

Reid's desk was littered with papers. When she came in, he pushed some of them aside and rose. The sleeves of his white shirt were rolled up to the elbow; his tie was loose, and a navy blazer lay across the back of a nearby chair. He started to unroll his sleeves, but Cassidy shook her head. 'Don't bother getting dressed,' she said, with a wry smile. 'My business isn't going to take more than a couple of minutes, and then you'd have it all to undo again.'

He grinned, but he didn't comment. 'Would you bring us coffee?' he asked the secretary. 'And then hold my calls.' He indicated a small sitting area in the corner of the room, where two small couches and a coffee-table on a lovely muted Persian area rug seemed to invite confidences.

Cassidy sat on the very edge of one of the couches. She was relieved when Reid relaxed opposite her, one arm stretched out over the back of the couch. He sat there silently, his coffee-cup casually palmed, as if he were free for the whole day, if she chose to use it.

She sipped her coffee and said, 'That's very good.'

'My secretary has had much more practice than you have,' Reid said gravely.

She coloured a little. Her couple of minutes, she reminded herself, were already gone. 'I suppose you want to know why I'm here.'

'It hadn't occurred to me. I was simply enjoying the view.'

'Come on, Reid—don't fence about things like that.' Irritation sharpened her voice, and she took a deep breath and calmed herself before going on. 'Are you seriously thinking of letting Chloe interview you, or were you just hoping I'd be too jealous to see straight, so I'd make any deal I had to?'

His eyebrows lifted. 'Jealous? You? What on earth would you have to be jealous of?'

It was like a slap in the face; the fact was that she had never thought of him as her exclusive property, and it irritated her that he thought she might.

'My story, Reid,' she said flatly. 'I was working on it first.'

'So you think you should have exclusive rights to it?'

'There is such a thing as professional etiquette, when two reporters work for the same newspaper——'

'But that's not my problem, is it?' His voice was almost silky.

'No. Your problem, if you talk to Chloe, is that she's a very good, very intense, very harsh reporter. She's not content with stories that brush the surface——'

He interrupted. 'And you are?'

'Of course not. But she has a habit of looking for scandal—well, perhaps scandal isn't a good way to put it, but everyone has a weakness, and Chloe has a talent for finding it. If you skipped out on a parking ticket in California ten years ago, for instance, she will know about it, and she'll draw conclusions from it about your character——'

'But you're not talking about parking tickets, are you, Cassidy? You're talking about you and me.'

'That's part of why I'm concerned,' Cassidy said honestly. 'Once she starts on you, she may ask the wrong questions. Don't forget she sent that money order from San Francisco.'

'Very bad judgement on your part.'

'I know. But that doesn't solve the problem now.'

'So what's your solution? That I should talk to you instead? I'm listening—convince me, Cassidy.'

'By telling you what I'm willing to do to persuade you?' She shook her head. 'My solution is much easier than that, Reid. I don't think you should talk to either of us. No story—period. You can't get any simpler than that, and since you don't like publicity anyway...'

She raised her coffee-cup as if it were the only thing she was interested in right now and watched him over the rim, through her lashes. She had hoped to see a flicker of surprise in his eyes, or a tell-tale tinge of colour rise over his lean cheeks; she hadn't quite expected the wave of shock that washed over his face, and then was quickly masked with a laugh. She watched with breathless interest. So she had found the elusive Mr Cavanaugh's weak spot, had she? And it looked like a deadly hit——

'You expect me to believe that, Cassidy? When you were practically clawing her eyes out a minute ago to protect your story?'

She smiled sweetly. 'You don't owe me anything. Besides, it wasn't my idea, in the first place,' she said. 'It was Brian's, and I'd be delighted to have a good excuse not to pursue it.'

She let him dangle for a long moment. Enjoy it, she told herself; you've never seen Reid Cavanaugh speechless before, and you're not likely to see it again.

Then, finally, she said, very gently, 'That's what I thought. I spent half the night trying to figure out what you're up to, you know. You want to do this interview, and you also want me to think I've talked you into doing it as a favour to me, but that's not the way it is at all—is it, Reid?'

He leaned forward as if intrigued by this new, amusing Cassidy. 'Now what makes you say that?'

Cassidy folded her arms across her chest and debated whether she should explain her reasoning.

'That doesn't help conceal your assets,' Reid murmured.

'Don't change the subject. It was something you said yesterday—I made a remark about your unions, and you asked if I'd been talking to your employees. That was quite a Freudian slip, Reid, letting me know that they're not happy with you just now. I started to wonder why, since there's never been a hint of trouble before. And that's when I realised that you want to get your side of it in the newspaper—without letting me know that I'm the one doing you a favour instead of the other way around.'

'Perhaps I should talk to Chloe,' he grumbled. 'She might be easier to handle after all.'

'Go right ahead.' She watched him for a long moment. 'So you don't need public relations campaigns, hmm? What's this, then?' She pulled the set of brochures out of her handbag and let them spill in a brilliant heap on the low table between the couches.

Reid shrugged. 'Marketing tools. They work very well, by the way. So why should I need reporters prying into my business, too?'

Cassidy gave him her most winning smile. 'My point exactly,' she murmured. 'Relax, Reid—you don't have to talk to anyone.' She set her cup aside, picked up her handbag, and was halfway to the door before he moved.

'Cassidy——'

She turned, with an enquiring eyebrow raised.

'Off the record——'

Cassidy shook her head. 'You say one more word, and it's for publication. You've had all the breaks you're going to get. Now, do you want to talk to me—or don't you?'

He sighed and ran his fingers through his hair. It looked good that way, she thought, thick and rumpled. 'If you don't want to do the story, Cassidy...'

She smiled, a little. 'I lied. Of course I want the story. And I forgot to tell you that I can be nearly as ruthless as Chloe can, when I'm not getting co-operation. And just as curious, too. If you talk to Chloe, I might just start talking to your employees.'

'Didn't you say something about professional etiquette a few minutes ago?'

'And then there will be two stories about you in the *Alternative*.'

'One will be plenty. It's quite a story.'

'Does that mean you want to tell me about it?'

'For all I know you may already have half of it,' he grumbled.

'That's possible,' she murmured. Her brain was running overtime, trying to figure out what she might know that she didn't know she knew. 'You may already have half of it'—but half of what?

'Oh, dammit, Cassidy,' he growled. 'Come back here and sit down.'

It *was* quite a story—or it would be, eventually; Reid made it perfectly plain that it was nothing more than speculation at the moment, until the negotiations were finished. And if anything interfered with those talks, the project would never come to pass, and then there would be no story at all.

Cassidy looked down at the blueprints spread across the low coffee-table. Her heart kept skittering from her throat to her diaphragm as she assessed all the possibilities. 'What a story!' she breathed.

Reid had leaned forward to point out something on the drawings; he drew back and his arm brushed hers. 'Not yet,' he warned. 'It's premature to release it.'

'I know, Reid. Remember? I agreed to hold off——'

'I'm just giving you background for now.'

'I understand—unless you and the unions reach a compromise, it may all come to nothing.'

'And if it weren't for that series of yours on the trouble young people are having getting into the housing market, I'd never have told you at all.' He looked at her accusingly. 'It was beginning to look to me as if I was going to see my most intimate business plans spread all over the front pages by next week at the latest.'

'Coincidence,' Cassidy said. 'I didn't have a clue.' But she sounded absent-minded; she was again studying the blueprints, the plans for an entirely new kind of

Cavanaugh condominiums. Still spacious, still elegantly sited, still with the kind of quality that he was known for—but at a price that even the first-time buyers could afford.

'All that talk of yours about how I'd have to wait and see what the rest of the series was about——' He sighed. 'And now you tell me that you forced my hand *by accident*?'

She looked up from the plans with a quick smile. 'Don't worry about it, Reid. It doesn't matter how I know about it, but now that I do——' Then she sobered at the doubtful look on his face. 'Don't get paranoid; I gave you my promise to wait, didn't I? Now tell me more about how you're going to make the finances work. Frankly, it looks impossible to me.' She glanced at her wristwatch and muffled a groan. 'No—don't even start. I have to get to the office right now, or Brian will be furious. Unless I can tell him about this...' It was tentative.

Reid shook his head emphatically. 'It's too soon, and there's too much of a chance that it will all come to nothing. The deal will certainly fall apart if there is any speculation in the newspapers.'

'There won't be. Brian's a professional; he knows when to sit on a story.'

'That may be true, but I'm certain of one thing: he can't print what he doesn't know.' It was firm. 'You'll have to keep it to yourself for the present, Cassidy.'

'And work on it on my own time,' she grumbled.

'Well, isn't that what good reporters do? There could be rewards, you know—shall we have dinner tonight at Amerigo's and I'll tell you all about it?'

'I can't get away tonight.'

He frowned. 'Don't tell me those sorority types can't practise their table manners without you for one evening.'

'Don't overestimate them. In any case, it is part of my job, you know.' She consulted her mental calendar. 'How about Saturday? I can get someone to fill in for me——'

He shook his head. 'I'm tied up then, I'm afraid.'

'I suppose that means you aren't going to give up a round of golf with the guys. Come on, Reid.' But she was a bit relieved, in a way. Saturday was a long way off, and the time to talk to a source was when the man was willing, not almost a week later, when he would have had plenty of time to think about the wisdom of talking at all. 'Then come over to the house tonight and we'll discuss it after dinner.'

'What time is dinner?'

'Seven o'clock. But——'

'I'll be there.' He stood up decisively, obviously ready to go back to work.

'That wasn't exactly what——' Cassidy paused and shrugged. 'Fine,' she said, with a fiendish smile. 'It will be good for the girls to have a male guest to practise on.'

He didn't flinch. 'I'm not worried. Haven't you forgotten something? I have it on the best authority that I don't even count as a male, where your girls are concerned.'

The young fools, Cassidy thought. They've got a lot of growing up to do!

But if the members of Alpha Chi thought that Reid Cavanaugh belonged to the geriatric set, there was no hint of it at the sorority house that night. The senior girl whose turn it was to act as hostess flirted with him throughout dinner, while Cassidy seethed at the far end of the table, longing for the opportunity to remind the girl of her manners. Afterwards, as everyone gathered for coffee and dessert in the parlour, the first year who was Reid's 'best authority' for his lack of status asked if he would like to attend the dance coming up on the weekend, and when he solemnly agreed that it might be fun Cassidy couldn't make up her mind which of them she'd like to scream at first.

But finally the last of the girls went off to their study hour, and Cassidy tried to conceal her sigh of relief as she said, 'Shall we get down to business, then? We won't be disturbed up in my sitting-room, short of the roof blowing off.'

Reid eyed the silver coffee-pot longingly. 'That's awfully good. May I have one more cup, to take upstairs with me?' Then he added solemnly, 'I wouldn't want to put you to the trouble of making some,' and she considered pouring it over his head.

Once in her sitting-room he settled himself comfortably in the corner of the love-seat, glared at the notebook that lay open on her knee, and said, 'That thing makes me nervous.'

'It just lets me keep the facts straight, Reid.'

'The facts aren't all that complicated. I'd be much more comfortable if we could just talk, and then when you get down to writing the article we can check the details——'

'Well, we aren't going to check details by letting you read my finished article, if that's what you have in mind,' she warned. 'I don't let anyone censor my stories.'

'Not even your editor?'

'That's a little different. Now—correct me if I'm wrong—you're asking your employees' unions for some concessions, to help hold down the prices of the finished condominiums. If they'll take a wage cut to work on these projects, they'll get a piece of the profits instead.'

He leaned back and sipped his coffee. 'They'll be stockholders in the company—which will give them an incentive to finish the job fast and efficiently and at a high quality level. In the end, the people who work on these units could end up making more money than union scale.'

She nodded. 'But to do that takes the permission of the union heads.'

Reid scowled. 'I don't like phrasing it that way. I'm not asking *permission*, exactly.'

She scratched out a note and wrote something else, looked at it for a moment, and said, 'All right, let's call it *approval*, then.'

'That's better.'

'And this will be decided—when?'

'Whenever all of us can get together in the same room to talk about it. Within the next few weeks, certainly. And no, you can't be there—you'd stick out a mile in that bunch of hard hats and three-piece legal ensembles. Take my word for it.'

She didn't argue the point; he was right, of course, and in any case there were all sorts of ways to get information. Instead she doodled a design on the edge of her notebook and thought about the whole scheme. The gentle creak of her rocking-chair formed a soft counterpoint to the pattern of her thoughts. Cutting costs on that massive scale, without sacrificing quality—it was going to take a great deal more than a concession from his unions to make this plan work, wasn't it?

She tried to frame the question, but before she could make it clear Reid asked, casually, 'How did Brian take it, by the way, when you came in two hours late this morning?'

Cassidy rolled her eyes. 'Not well,' she said. 'And yes, I did manage to soothe him without explaining to him where I'd been. You owe me something for that.'

'I'll think it over and see if I can come up with something appropriate. Normally I'd offer you an evening out, but of course I understand why you don't wish to be separated from your charming house-mates for a single evening.'

'Don't be snide, Cavanaugh. One of the benefits of sorority life is a civilised dinner-table conversation, and someone has to set the example. Besides, you're the one who agreed to come to the dance——'

'No, I didn't. I just said it might be fun.'

'Close enough. And if you don't understand why someone has to be here——'

'Of course I know someone has to do it. What I don't understand is why it has to be you. Doesn't it get tiresome, Cassidy?'

'Oh, sometimes I'd like to have a little more free time. But it's not as if my duties are overwhelming, anyway. I don't set up the rules or discipline anyone for violating them; the girls' own governing council does that. I just give the place a little tone, and a bit of chaperonage, and——'

'Is the chaperoning for the girls' sake, or yours, Cassidy?'

'What?' She stopped rocking suddenly and looked at him in shock. 'I haven't exactly slept my way through the male population of Kansas City, if that's what you're implying——'

He finished his coffee and set the cup and saucer down on the lamp table with a firm click. 'I'd say you never even had a good start.'

She stared at him for a long moment. 'Would you mind explaining to me why that sounded like an insult, Cavanaugh?'

'Did it? I didn't mean it that way, exactly. I just meant that being a house-mother certainly makes things easier for you. You have a built-in excuse not to go out, not to see men——'

'I told you before, I'm not interested. Kent was special.'

'Are you so certain of that? Or are you afraid, deep down, that if you date a few other men you might find out Kent wasn't so exceptional after all?'

She simply stared at him, not quite certain if she was hearing correctly.

'I loved my little brother, Cassidy, but I wasn't blinded by his faults. Kent was a selfish, spoiled child who lived only for the pleasure of the moment——'

'Stop it!'

'Don't you like hearing the truth? I thought you prided yourself on discovering it, no matter how painful—or does that only apply to other people's lives, and not your own?' He got to his feet as if he simply couldn't sit still any longer. 'Are you afraid that, if you look around, you might find someone who could drive Kent out of your mind? Is that the real reason why you've buried yourself here?'

It took raw effort to keep herself from shrinking down into a heap in the corner of her rocking-chair as he stood over her. She gathered the last bits of her poise. 'I'm not admitting anything,' she said curtly. 'But even if that were all true, what business is it of yours, Reid?'

He didn't answer right away. He walked across the room to stare out of the window, and said, over his shoulder, 'Because you're using me as an excuse, Cassidy.'

'I beg your pardon?'

He turned to face her. 'The money,' he said softly. 'As long as you tell yourself you have to work at this job to pay me back, you don't have to look at the real reason.'

She jumped up. 'What you're calling *the real reason* is nonsense, Reid!'

'Then prove it,' he challenged. 'Stop sending the money—you don't owe me a cent, and you never did. Quit this job. Start living again, instead of pretending——'

'I don't have to prove anything to you.' She steadied her voice and smiled, with an effort. 'We seem to have wandered a long way from the subject, don't we?' She retrieved her notebook from the carpet and settled herself in the rocking-chair again. 'You were telling me about the financing on this deal—how you were going to hold the prices down, without sacrificing quality.'

He didn't seem to hear her. He watched her for a long time; his eyes were half closed, but there was nothing lazy about his gaze. 'That look of yours,' he mused. 'That serene, peaceful look you've got—as if nothing ever bothers you. It started out as a mask to hide your private pain, but somewhere along the way you must have forgotten that you were wearing it, and let it become part of you. I would like to rip that mask away from you, Cassidy—to make you feel again...'

For a long moment the air in the sitting-room seemed to crackle with tension. Then Cassidy said, pleasantly, 'I'm afraid you're mistaken.'

He shook his head. 'No, I'm not mistaken. I remember you when the mask was new, when it still slipped sometimes. And I knew Kent very well indeed.'

She didn't want to ask, but the words seemed to force themselves out. 'What has that got to do with anything?'

'The girls he lived with were a varied lot——'

Cassidy was gripping her pen so hard that her fingers ached. The emphasis on the plural, she thought, was quite deliberate.

'—but the one thing they weren't was serene and peaceful and calm.'

'Do you know because you tracked them all down and checked them out?' she said tightly. 'Or should I feel honoured that you made a special case of me?'

'I didn't make you a special case,' he said slowly. 'You did that yourself, don't you think?'

It was like a dash of cold water in her face. How, she asked herself desperately, how for one instant could you have forgotten about the baby? 'This mask I supposedly wear,' she said. 'I suppose you think it's your mission in life to undo it?' She shook her head. 'You're not being very wise, you know, Reid. You've given me a great deal of sensitive information today——'

'And you'd blackmail me with it? I don't think so. You want this story too much to take chances with it.'

'It's true that I want the story.' She kept her voice steady. 'And I'll do the story—either with your co-operation or behind your back. Which would you prefer?'

He smiled, a little. Suddenly businesslike, he said, 'You were asking, I believe, how I plan to build quality housing for a third of the price it normally costs?' He raised one hand, fingers outstretched as if he was ready to start ticking off points.

Cassidy realised that she had been holding her breath, and quietly released it.

Abruptly, Reid stopped talking and put his hands on his hips. His head was tilted a bit to one side as he studied her, and finally he said, almost gently, 'That sounded like relief. Why, Cassidy? Could it be because you know, in your heart, that I'm right?'

'Have you always had this tendency to tell people how to live, or am I the only one who brings out the worst in you?'

He didn't answer, but she thought that the question had startled him.

'Make up your mind, Reid. You can have my co-operation on this story, or the doubtful pleasure of trying to reform my life—but you can't have both. So you'd better decide which you want.' She clipped her pen neatly to the edge of her notebook and rose. 'Let me know what you decide, please. Now, I really must see what the girls are up to in the ballroom—heaven knows what wild schemes they'll come up with next.'

The dismissal seemed to amuse him, and for an instant she thought he was going to refuse to leave the room. 'Ah, yes,' he said. 'Your girls need you. Don't feel you have to walk me to the front door.'

She didn't; she collapsed into the rocking-chair again as soon as the door closed softly behind him, and she sat there as the sound of his footsteps faded away as he descended the stairs. But the echo of his voice stayed with her.

'As long as you tell yourself you have to work at this job to pay me back, you don't have to look at the real reason.'

She was tired; that was why her brain seemed fuzzy and achy all of a sudden. She had been carrying a heavy load for the last few months, with two jobs that demanded time and devotion and concentration. Summer would be easier; there would be fewer girls living in the house, and the schedule would be lighter. She was looking forward to the break between the spring and summer terms, too—two weeks when she would have no

duties at the house, when she would not have to carefully plan her time or balance her responsibilities with
such care.

'Quit this job. Start living again, instead of pretending——'

He's a fool, she thought. The real reason, indeed! I'm
not avoiding men, or anything at all—it's just that I can't
feel free as long as I owe that debt.

And even with this second job, it was going to take a
long time till it was all behind her; she would be past
thirty by the time the last payment was made...

It had never seemed such a horribly long time to wait,
before.

CHAPTER SIX

CASSIDY propped her elbows on her desk, her fingertips resting on her temples to support the weight of her head—which seemed, today, to be about half a ton. A yellow notebook lay open on the blotter in front of her. On it were just a few words, neatly printed in a straight, careful list—mostly the names of people who might know something about Reid Cavanaugh's new scheme, or who might know someone else who did. It was a very short list, and that was part of the reason her head ached. It was mid-afternoon, and it was increasingly apparent that Reid intended to call her bluff; he'd already had nearly a full day to make contact with her, but obviously he didn't plan to do any such thing. Now she was going to have to come up with the story on her own, or look like a fool for threatening to do something she couldn't carry out.

It wasn't that she cared so much about looking like a fool, she told herself. But it was still an incredible story, and she couldn't just ignore it. On the other hand, she couldn't publish half of it, either—and she couldn't seem to think of anyone who might actually know the rest.

She stared at the neat list of names. Brian had had the right idea in sending her to that cocktail party to make the proper connections with important people, she thought, but it was too bad he hadn't done it a year ago!

You're not thinking clearly, she told herself firmly. You're exhausted from helping the girls decorate last night, and a little panicky over the fact that what could be a prize-winning story is slipping through your fingers. That's all——

As if, she told herself bitterly, that wasn't enough! If Reid had actually planned this he couldn't have set her up so neatly——

The thought stopped her cold. Was that, perhaps, exactly what he had done? Had she stepped into an unseen, even deeper trap, at the very moment she had been priding herself on her own cleverness?

She thought about that for a while, and then shook her head. No, the story couldn't have been a plant; he'd been deadly serious about the whole thing. And what possible reason could Reid have for wanting to publicly embarrass her? It would certainly backfire on him, as well...

You're so tired that you're beginning to become paranoid, she told herself. Another couple of weeks and the pressure will let up. You'll have time to take deep breaths again, and walks, and maybe even a shopping trip——

Damn Reid anyway, she thought. The mere suggestion that she was working herself to a frazzle for no good reason had seemed to act on her tired mind in an almost hypnotic manner, making everything seem just that much worse. In the months she had been a house-mother, she had never even considered resigning from the job—but after Reid's comments last night she had awakened in the small hours to find herself thinking how nice it would be to have a place of her own again, and no one else to be responsible for...

'You look as if you were out all night.' Chloe McPherson put down the telephone at the next desk and wheeled her chair around to face Cassidy. 'Doesn't the curfew at that place apply to you, too?'

'Unfortunately, there's a difference between curfew and lights-out, and last night we were painting galaxies till the wee hours.'

'Galaxies?' Chloe looked as if she thought Cassidy had finally lost her mind completely.

'You know, scenery for the dance. I don't know how the other house-mothers do it,' Cassidy mused. 'The one next door is past seventy. She's such a sweet and motherly type that I'd like to cry on her shoulder myself sometimes, but how she ever keeps up with the girls——'

'Perhaps she lets them paint their own galaxies. I'd like to talk to you some time, Cassidy.'

Cassidy became very intent on the new lead she was inserting in her mechanical pencil. 'Oh? What about?'

'Your friend Reid Cavanaugh.'

So he was going to talk to Chloe after all. She kept her voice carefully casual. 'Background for a story?'

'Some day, maybe. I'm intrigued by the man. Nobody's got a bad thing to say about him——'

'I should think that would make him a fairly boring subject.' Despite the seriousness of the conversation, Cassidy almost had to stifle a smile as she said it. Reid—boring? No, he was hardly that——

'I always wonder about people like that, though. Nobody can honestly be perfect, and I'd just like to know what makes him tick. That scholarship fund of yours, for instance——'

Cassidy couldn't help it; she cringed a little. 'Damn,' she said quickly. 'I always manage to stab myself at least once, changing the lead in this stupid pencil.' She stuck her fingertip in her mouth, certain that Chloe wouldn't insist on inspecting the supposed wound.

A long shadow fell across her desk, and she looked up with foreboding. But the uniformed man who stood there was one she had never seen before. His dark burgundy coat bore a neat emblem on the breast pocket, and he carried a crisp shopping bag with a snappy white and burgundy design on the side. 'Miss Adams? I have a delivery for you from the Gourmandi Grocery.' He set the bag down on her blotter with a smile and an elegant bow, and was off again before she could even mumble her thanks.

Chloe hadn't stopped talking. 'Was it just a good deed, or is there more reason than that for it. How many people has he put through college? And——'

'Sure—we'll talk about him some time,' Cassidy said, trying to sound casual. She added to herself, I'm sure I can find a few minutes for you in a decade or two, Chloe.

Meanwhile, she eyed the bag with suspicion; she certainly hadn't ordered anything from Gourmandi, the most élite and expensive food shop in the city. She peeked inside; the bag held a half-gallon jar of speciality olives.

The sudden silence from the next desk caught Cassidy's attention. Chloe was staring at the contents of the bag. 'I'm obviously only a peasant,' she said. 'When I think of take-out food, my mind runs to pizza and moo shue pork—not olives in quantity. Unless, of course, there's a half-gallon of gin in there, too, and a little vermouth.'

Martini makings—of course, Cassidy thought. This was the brand of olives that could be bought only at Gourmandi, the kind they'd been using in the martinis at the cocktail party that night at the Cottage. The kind she had told Reid she liked.

'There's no gin,' she said. 'Sorry, Chloe.'

There was also no card, but then she didn't need that; only Reid could have sent her the olives. The thing that puzzled her was why. Was it some sort of making-up gesture? Or was it a challenge instead? Obviously she was supposed to read some sort of message into this, but it defeated her to know what it was.

'What a lost opportunity,' Chloe said mournfully, her questions about Reid momentarily forgotten.

Cassidy seized her chance and rushed out of the building, muttering something over her shoulder about a forgotten appointment, before Chloe had a chance to return to her original topic.

I might not be able to avoid the problem entirely, but at least, Cassidy thought, I can have a bit of peace first to think up some good excuses for not talking about Reid—excuses which will stand up to Chloe's probing.

Though on the other hand, she thought, perhaps it might be just as well if I don't try very hard at all. It would serve him right if Chloe and I collaborated!

She was in the kitchen negotiating a compromise between the members of the entertainment committee, who had created a list of gourmet goodies they couldn't do without at the dance, and the cook, who had to produce those goodies on top of her regular work, when the door swung open and a high-pitched girl's voice announced, 'Cassidy! Your favourite man is here!'

Heather strikes again, Cassidy thought with resignation as the girl appeared in the swinging door with a man behind her—a tall man with salt-and-pepper hair, wearing a grey tweed sports jacket.

Then Heather put a confiding hand on Reid's arm and looked up at him earnestly. 'Since we call Cassidy Mom,' she murmured, 'it feels awfully odd to have you be Mr Cavanaugh. Shall we just start calling you Daddy, or would you prefer your first name? A lot of stepfathers do, I know——'

'That's *enough*,' Cassidy said, and concluded from Heather's expression that she had reacted precisely as the girl hoped she would. She bit her tongue, but it was too late.

Heather grinned and slithered out of the room, and Cassidy was left glaring at Reid, who seemed incapable of taking a hint. Instead, he graciously accepted the cup of coffee that the cook pressed on him, sampled one of the tiny barbecued meatballs that had caused the kitchen conference in the first place, and settled himself on a high stool in the middle of the room as if prepared to enjoy the discussion forever.

Cassidy lost her temper. 'I'm sure I don't care what you have to eat Saturday night,' she told the entertainment committee. 'If you want the fancy things, then you'll have to pitch in and help make them. Is that clear?'

The girls, obviously startled by the unusual sharpness in her voice, meekly agreed, and Cassidy turned to face Reid. 'And what do you want?'

'A private word with you, perhaps?' he murmured.

'To say what?'

Reid's eyebrows arched. 'Didn't you get my apology?'

'Is that what it was. It looked like a jar of olives to me.' She sounded cross, but inside she didn't know what to feel—relief? Pleasure? Irritation? 'Besides, what makes you think I'm interested in an apology from you, no matter how it's phrased?'

He smiled a little. 'Oh, you're interested. Would you rather I drop to my knees? I will, if you insist, but it would cause talk. Much better to do it in private.'

She gave up. 'Oh, come upstairs—you'll end up there, anyway. I suppose if I was in the shower, they'd still show you straight in——'

'Do you think so?' It was sober, thoughtful. 'In that case, Cassidy, when do you generally take your showers?'

She glared at him.

Once in her sitting-room, he closed the door, leaned against it, and said rapidly, 'You were right last night; I was trying to run your life and tell you what to do, and it's none of my business. If I promise not to say anything more about the money, will you please forgive me?'

There was a tremor in his voice. Cassidy thought it was suspiciously artistic. 'Not another word?' she said.

He shook his head meekly. 'Not one.'

She let him dangle for half a minute, and then she said, 'All right. It's a truce. But——'

The tremor vanished. 'Then let's get down to work on the story again,' he said briskly.

It left her with an odd, let-down feeling. It shouldn't, she told herself. You've known since yesterday how important that story is to him—certainly it's far more significant in his mind than your attitudes about debts! Once he got away from here last night and calmed down, he realised that, and so did you—so it certainly shouldn't surprise you now.

'The next time you want to apologise, Reid,' she began, her voice deliberately light.

'Don't count on it being a regular event, now.'

'Instead of olives, please send giant cashew nuts. Tyler-Royale has the best ones in town, in their candy department.' She tugged her notebook out, in defiance of his disapproving look.

But he didn't say anything, this time, about her taking notes. 'Have you always been such a connoisseur of junk food?' he asked.

'Yes. I cut my baby teeth on jawbreakers. Now about the price of these condos...'

She thought there was the merest flicker in his eyes, as there sometimes was when someone was reluctant to tell the entire truth. But if it was there, it very quickly vanished, and in the next half-hour, as he detailed his plans, she dismissed the idea altogether. He had laid everything out; for the life of her she couldn't find anything missing.

Finally she leaned back in her chair, closed her eyes, and said, 'It really is a new approach, isn't it?'

'Not altogether. I've just put together elements from all kinds of schemes that have been tried before—with varying success.'

'Still——'

'There have been factory-built homes for years. I've adopted a great many of their assembly-line techniques, but I'm going to do the building on the site instead of in a factory.'

'Using less skilled labour.'

'It takes less skill to do it that way.'

'In other words, cheaper labour.'

'That goes along with it, yes.'

'And that's why your unions aren't very enthusiastic about the idea.'

'I'd say they're wary at the moment of a two-level pay scale. What they haven't seen yet is how many more units we can build this way, and, because of these new methods, we can practically wipe out the seasonal lay-offs that have always been a problem in the construction trade. A carpet-layer can't work year-round unless there are floors for him to work on. We'll be building twice the number of floors, so——'

She doodled a flower on the corner of her notebook. 'Why are you doing this, Reid?'

His eyes narrowed. 'I don't quite see what you mean.'

'What's in it for you? Obviously there's not a lot of money to be made.'

'Not per unit, no. But multiplied——'

Cassidy shook her head. 'Not compared to the investment you're making. So why do it?'

He was silent for a long time, and then he said, slowly, 'Some of my own employees are caught in that squeeze you wrote about—they can't afford to buy the condominiums they build.'

'But surely that's not your problem. There is no shortage of people to buy your expensive line—so why take such a big chance for so little return?'

'That doesn't sound like you, Cassidy.'

'If you don't like the question,' she murmured, 'be glad you didn't talk to Chloe.'

He smiled, then. 'Are you still worrying about what insights she might find into my character? Don't. My secretary called her this afternoon, and told her that I just couldn't fit her into my busy season, but perhaps in the fall I'd have time for an interview. So you can put Chloe out of your mind.'

'I'm glad you didn't just refuse her,' Cassidy said quietly. 'Chloe can be—I don't know—hard, somehow. And she seems worse just now. I hope it will be better when she gets back into the routine of work, but I can't help wondering——' She stopped. There was a tiny sketch in the margin of her notebook—a stick figure of a child. She didn't remember drawing it.

'Wondering what?'

'If it's Theresa.' It was soft, as if she were talking to herself. 'Her little girl,' she explained. 'Chloe wants to work, but I can't help thinking that she must feel horribly guilty about leaving that child when she doesn't have to—they've been doing fine without her income. That was one of the reasons——' She stopped herself, abruptly, feeling as if she had suddenly awakened to find herself standing on the lip of a precipice, swaying over the edge, without the slightest idea of how she had got there or how to regain her balance.

'That was one of the reasons——?' Reid prompted.

Cassidy shrugged. 'Oh, it was nothing—who am I to judge Chloe, anyway?'

There was a silence, and after a moment she dared to look up at him, smiling brightly, intending to say something light and flippant about how she was such an authority on mothering, now that she had thirty-two girls of her own to look after. But the compassion that she saw in his eyes, turning the grey almost to black, seized her by the throat and paralysed her vocal cords. She had not anticipated that empathy, from him ...

'That was why you were willing to let Fudge go,' he said. It was not a question.

She tried to laugh. 'I thought you'd forgotten that silliness.'

There was a look of disbelief in his face. 'Forgotten Fudge? How on earth could I forget——?'

No, he had not forgotten the pain, she thought. Or the mess it had all been. And perhaps, sometimes, he too still thought of the promise of a new life full of possibilities—a promise that had been so cruelly cut short.

'Not the baby, I don't mean you'd forgotten him. But the name——' She could feel her control slipping, and yet she couldn't stop herself. 'All that nonsense...' But it hadn't been nonsense to her, and suddenly she was crying, great, shattering sobs that racked her body.

'Cassidy——' He was beside her, half crouched on the floor next to her chair, his hand on her shoulder. 'I'm sorry—I'm so very sorry I reminded you.'

'Reminded me?' She glared at him. 'As if *everything* doesn't remind me! Every time I see a baby, or——'

The words were choked and nearly incoherent. She threw her notebook aside almost viciously, and rummaged for a tissue. He pressed a big white handkerchief into her fingers, and the bulk and the softness of it made her cry harder, as if he had handed her a baby's dainty blanket.

Then suddenly she was in his arms, being rocked as if she were only a child herself. She buried her face in his shoulder, and he whispered, against her temple, 'It's all right. Cry it out, Cassidy. Cry it all out...'

So she did, held close against the solid warmth of him, secure for the moment with the comforting vibration of his heart beneath her cheek. And when finally there were no more tears to shed she gave one last little whimpering sob and whispered, 'All this time, it's been as if he was never truly real—there was no one I could talk to——'

'You've never even told anyone about him?'

She shook her head. 'Have you?' she asked quietly.

'No—but——'

'But it's different?' she said sadly. 'Perhaps it was, for you.' And she might have believed it, if she hadn't looked up at him just then, and recognised that the expression in Reid's eyes was a mirror reflection of her own pain. Had he, too, truly mourned—not just for Kent's child, but for Fudge's own sake?

It was so very natural to raise her hand to his cheek, to try to comfort him. And when he bent his head to kiss her—well, that was a simple gesture of comfort too, wasn't it?

But comforting kisses were not supposed to induce this odd helplessness, like the paralysis of a dream state, that left her unable to do anything but lie quietly in his arms. Comforting kisses were not intended to set fire to the very centre of a woman's being. Comforting kisses were not supposed to be confusing ones...

She told herself that all the time he kissed her, while the taste of him seemed to trickle through her veins till each cell was a-quiver with it. And then she gave up thinking at all, and simply released herself to the pleasure he was giving her, the mindless sensations that sent her brain reeling.

When finally he stopped kissing her, and very gently took his arms from around her, she was stunned at the way that her body rebelled against the sudden withdrawal of warmth and support and sensation. If he had actually made love to her, and then walked out on her without a word, it could not have been a greater shock than this——

She ducked her head to hide the sudden flare of embarrassed colour in her cheeks, and Reid looked at her quizzically for a long moment and then went over to the tiny sink to wet a towel in cold water.

He handed it to her without a word, and Cassidy tried to laugh. 'I must be one giant blotch,' she said, and began to pat at her face.

'You're feeling better, if you're worried about how you look.' But he sounded almost absent-minded.

'Thank you for calling a halt to that,' she said.

'I thought it was time, before things got out of hand.'

It was matter-of-fact, and Cassidy's eyes dropped. 'I'm sorry,' she said. 'I don't quite know what came over me, but I assure you I had no intention of——'

'Of taking advantage of me? That's funny; I was just about to say the same thing to you.'

'Well, that's certainly a relief.' It was just a little tart, and she didn't look at him as she said it. She crossed the room and spread the towel out over the edge of the sink to dry, being very careful to line it up just so.

'Cassidy——' But he stopped there, as if he didn't quite know what to say.

Her head was starting to ache. Good lord, Cassidy, she told herself. A simple comforting kiss, and you tried to turn it into a one-night stand. The man didn't even put a hand on you anywhere that a brother wouldn't——

A brother. For a little while, she had forgotten all about Kent. But it was obvious that Reid had not.

It was almost a relief when there was a knock on the door. Cassidy called, 'Come in,' and Heather put her head in the door. Cassidy thought she looked a bit disappointed at the perfectly platonic scene inside.

'We're trying out some more new ideas for the ballroom,' Heather said. 'Will you come up and look?'

'Certainly. I'll be right there.' She glanced at Reid. 'They keep dreaming up these last-minute changes in plans, and if I don't go up and keep them in check——'

'Convenient,' Reid murmured. 'Was it difficult to train them to interrupt any time you've got a guest?'

Her temper snapped. 'Look, Reid, you promised not to bring that up again——'

'I promised not to say anything more about the money.'

'It's the same thing,' she said stubbornly. 'This may take a while; don't feel you have to wait for me.'

'Oh, I know better than to do that.' It was very smooth. He gathered up his jacket.

Her remark had come out more sharply than Cassidy had intended, and as she walked him down to the front door she tried to soften it. 'Honestly, I wasn't trying to get rid of you. I just meant that I expect you've got other things to do——'

He smiled, a little. 'A few dozen. Let me know when you need to talk about details, Cassidy. And I'll call you if there's anything new.'

Then he was gone, into the night.

And it was utterly stupid of her to feel forlorn and friendless, all of a sudden. It was only the night-chilled air, she told herself. It certainly was nothing personal, nothing to do with him. He'd kissed her, that was all. So why was she making such a big deal of it?

Because you didn't want him to stop, her conscience replied, and she leaned against the deep-carved walnut doorway with her hands pressed against her temples, trying to still that insistent little whisper. But the voice could not be silenced, for it was speaking the truth. You'd have enjoyed letting him make love to you, if that was what he had wanted . . .

The realisation rocked her to the core. For four years she had done without physical intimacy, and told herself that she no longer needed or wanted to feel those uncomfortable longings. But now her body was reminding her that those hungers had not died after all, but had only gone to sleep for a while. And once awakened——

It was a most unwelcome discovery.

She went up to the attic ballroom and listened to the girls' newest scheme, to hook up spotlights in every corner to highlight the stars and the clouds that now lined the ceiling, and shook her head.

'Too much lighting invites inspection,' she told them. 'Sometimes it's better to leave things a bit mysterious, and just enjoy the atmosphere while you can.'

Finally, reluctantly, the girls gave up the notion, but it was after midnight by the time she undressed in the dark and slipped into her bed.

That's good, she told herself. This way I'm much too tired to worry about lying awake tonight, thinking about—things.

At least be honest, she told herself. It isn't things in general that are bothering you; you just don't want to think about Reid, the source of that blinding, embarrassing illumination. Thank heaven, she thought, that he hadn't read her reaction and realised how easily she would have agreed to go to bed with him——

But he had known. He must have known.

The sudden understanding was like a blow to her solar plexus, forcing all the air out of her lungs with a sudden, overwhelming pain. The man wasn't inexperienced—he was obviously no novice at the fine art of kissing, for example. And she refused to believe that a man of Reid's stamp would never have had an affair. He was discreet, yes—but that was a long way from being passionless.

So, obviously, he had known what she was inviting. 'At the rate you were putting out signals,' she told herself, 'you were probably glowing.'

But he had not acted on that invitation. Instead, he had released himself and handed her a wet towel—a *towel*!

'Suggesting a cold shower might have been less tactful, but more appropriate,' she told herself bitterly.

Once he had said to her, 'I would like to rip that mask away...to make you feel again——'

But she had given him that invitation tonight, and he had not acted on it. Instead he had seized the opportunity to get away. He'd been practically running——

She buried her face in her pillow, and the heat of her humiliation warmed the feathers all the way through to where her hands were clenched painfully tight against the mattress.

She told herself that she should be so angry at this rejection that she would never want to see him again. But it wasn't true. She told herself that she should be grateful that he had been too much the gentleman to take advantage of a woman he didn't care about. But it didn't help. The fact that he had walked away from her only made the longing worse.

She lay there in the cool, forgiving darkness and admitted that her longing had not been some momentary aberration. She still wanted him to touch her in all the intimate ways there were, until she could no longer draw breath or think of anything but their mutual pleasure. She wanted him to hold her, to caress her, to share with her the private, secret world of lovers...

CHAPTER SEVEN

CASSIDY had always liked to work as far in advance as possible, to be as ready as any human could be for the sudden breaks and surprises that were bound to occur in the news business. She had learned from harsh experience to assemble the sections of a story as she went along, rather than waiting till all the pieces were in hand and then writing it in one grand session, because she could more easily see the gaps and discover the questions that still needed to be asked. And often—if it was necessary—she could finish a story in an hour or two, whenever the last bits of information became available. On occasion, that ahead-of-time work had meant the difference between making the *Alternative*'s deadline and waiting another day, which sometimes meant letting another newspaper beat her to the story altogether—the cardinal sin of reporting.

So by Friday, much of the difficult, detailed, patient fitting-together of facts was finished, and an unfinished draft of the story was safely buried in the bottom drawer of her desk. The story lacked a lead, of course; she had jotted down some ideas, but the final version would have to wait for the outcome of the negotiations. And there were still holes to be filled—there were great gaps, for instance, where the reactions of union leaders would be added, after the dealing was done. And there were missing details which only Reid could provide.

'Let me know when you need to talk about details,' he had said. But she hadn't tried to call him. At the newspaper office, it seemed that the very moment she

112

worked up her nerve and picked up the telephone, Chloe turned around from her nearby desk to make a comment, or Brian summoned her to his office, or another reporter walked by. And in the evening, the Alphas and their press of last-minute work were keeping her on her toes. Besides, was it any wonder that she didn't particularly want to call Reid at the Cottage, in case his mother answered the telephone?

Oh, at least be honest with yourself, she lectured on Friday morning as she stared at the computer screen and tried to write a very ordinary story that simply would not come together in her mind. It isn't Reid's mother that bothers you, really, though of course you're not likely to ever be her favourite confidante. It's Reid himself, and that damned embarrassing kiss, and the way you reacted to it——

All right, she told herself firmly. So you discovered, to your discomfort, that you aren't entirely frozen after all. It was a crazy physical reaction, that's all.

It was annoying, of course, that Reid had turned out to be right, and that the instant she had let herself get close to a man she began to feel things again. But that didn't make it *personal*, for heaven's sake. Sometimes people had the oddest reactions to other people; finding someone physically attractive was not a crime, and it certainly didn't mean more than that. She was an adult, and when these things happened adults shrugged them off and went on with life.

And so she would, too, Cassidy told herself, and the next time that Chloe left her desk she called Reid's office. His secretary told her he was out for the day and that she was not expecting him back at all until Monday, when she would certainly give him a message.

Cassidy left her message, but every ounce of reporter's instinct was quivering when she put the telephone down.

He was not only out of the office, but out of touch as well. The only thing she could think of which would account for that was the meeting on which every aspect of this new project hinged. But he had said he would call her if there was anything new to report——

But he had made it very plain that she could not be a part of the conference herself. And he hadn't promised that he would tell her ahead of time, she reminded herself. Though what had he expected her to do if she knew about the meeting, anyway? she asked herself in annoyance. Dress up like a CIA spy and lurk in the corridors?

She seemed to remember that he had said he would not be free on Saturday. She had assumed that he would be playing golf, but he had never explained what he would be doing, so it was quite reasonable to assume that he had known, even then, that this was the weekend when it would all come to a head——

That was careless, she told herself. Your antennae must have been out of order that day!

'That must be quite a story,' Chloe said, coming back to her desk with a fresh can of pop. 'The way you're scowling at it, it's obviously of earth-shattering importance.'

'It's certainly important to the people involved,' Cassidy said. But it brought her back to earth a bit, and she made up her mind to be more careful around the office. There was no sense in trying to do anything where she might be overheard.

If Reid was in a conference somewhere, his secretary would gladly suffer torture before she admitted his whereabouts, Cassidy was certain. But there were other ways to get information. There was, for instance, the housekeeper at the Cottage. Cassidy and Mrs Miller had always got along rather well...

That was why, on Saturday morning, when Cassidy's assistant suggested that she looked as if she needed a day off, she jumped at the opportunity, and drove out to Mission Hills before she could have a chance to think it over and talk herself out of it.

The Cottage lay quiet under a golden blanket of sunshine. A honey-bee buzzed drowsily among the snow-white blooms of the pear tree in front of the dining-room window as Cassidy approached the kitchen door. The insect was the only sign of life——

From behind a burning bush at the corner of the house a head appeared, looking something like a Cheshire cat, and for a moment Cassidy wasn't sure whether to stop and chat, or scream and run. What sort of lunatic would be lurking behind the bushes?

Then the head, half-hidden by a floppy hat, was followed by a pair of hands wearing gardening gloves and holding pruning shears. At least it wasn't a lunatic, Cassidy reflected—only Reid's mother, which might actually end up to be worse.

She had never seen Jenna Cavanaugh so closely before. The lovely patrician face of the photographs was now showing the creeping signs of age, but Cassidy had the feeling that Jenna did not intend to surrender this battle lightly. She looked, Cassidy thought, as if she did not give up on anything without a struggle.

'May I help you?' The tone of voice was slightly autocratic, as if Jenna Cavanaugh was not accustomed to having to confront casual passers-by at her back door. But as Cassidy turned to face her directly, sunlight caught against her red-gold hair, and the challenge died out of the woman's voice. 'You're Cassidy, aren't you?'

Cassidy saw no reasonable way to deny it. I'm caught, she thought ruefully. And what do I say now? I can't exactly claim a bosom friendship with Mrs Miller. And I'd rather not tell her I'm spying on Reid, either.

Jenna Cavanaugh smiled, and the forbidding sternness of her face dissolved. The wrinkles beside her mouth became smile lines, and the harsh angles of her jaw softened. 'Reid told you, then, that I'd like to talk to you? Let me get rid of these tools and wash my hands, and we'll make some coffee and have a chat.'

Before Cassidy could gather her wits, she had been swept into the kitchen, and Jenna was dealing competently with a state-of-the-art coffee-maker and chatting gently, without a pause.

Why, she isn't strict and sober after all, Cassidy thought. She's sad—and perhaps a bit lonely. She must have softened a little, with the years.

The kitchen was spotless, as always. Jenna seemed to be very much at home in it, and there was no sign of Mrs Miller. Cassidy asked about her, as Jenna organised a tray with snow-white linen and old rose-patterned china and a plate of exquisite tiny cookies.

'Heavens, no, she hasn't left—Reid could never manage without her,' Jenna said. 'She's doing some last-minute marketing this morning. Let's have our coffee on the veranda, shall we? It's such a beautiful morning that I hate to be indoors.' She fussed over Cassidy, making sure she was comfortable. 'I'll miss her a great deal, of course.'

Cassidy blinked in confusion.

Jenna poured their coffee and looked up. 'Oh, dear, that must sound odd. I'm so excited about my new little nest, you see, that I forget not everyone in the world knows about it.'

'You're moving?'

Jenna nodded. 'I've bought an apartment in the Walnuts. You know, near Country Club Plaza.'

Cassidy nodded; everybody knew the Walnuts, probably the most exclusive and expensive apartment complex in the city. It was even more exclusive, she thought a bit cynically, than Reid's top-quality condominiums, and Jenna was obviously not allowing maternal prejudice to influence her when it came to investing in property!

'I thought Reid said you were quite happy at the Cottage,' she said, and then wanted to choke herself, because it was certainly none of her concern.

'Oh, Reid and I have got along beautifully. But—well, there comes a time when a mother in the house makes one too many women.'

And that, Cassidy thought, made it all too perfectly clear. 'He's thinking of being married, I suppose.' She was proud of her steady voice. Irrationally so, she thought; it should have been no surprise that Reid wanted a normal marriage, perhaps children of his own——

Jenna's cup hovered over the delicate saucer for several seconds. 'He's certainly said nothing specific to me,' she said finally.

And that, Cassidy thought, was hardly a firm denial. Yes, Jenna knew—and she was making sure that Cassidy knew, too.

'I'll miss the garden, of course,' Jenna said. It was a conventional, safe, social comment. She waved a hand at the green expanse of lawn behind the house, studded with trees bursting into bloom and flower-beds creeping into exotic life. 'I can't move until fall, when the apartment's ready, so it will be all right this year. But I don't know what will happen to it after that.'

It amused Cassidy, a little. 'Reid must like all the plants or he wouldn't have had them put in. Surely——'

'That's true. But his lawn service just isn't quite the thing. A garden needs personal care, and Reid is simply too busy with other things to pay attention. Today, for example—it's a perfect day, and what is he doing?' But it was purely a rhetorical question; she stopped there, and shook her head sadly.

Cassidy wanted to scream. Take it very gently, she told herself. It's obvious that she knows, and if you handle it just right she'll tell you where he is. 'Let me guess,' she said, her voice carefully casual. 'Is he playing racketball or something? Or does he work on Saturdays as well?'

'Work.' Jenna sniffed. 'Oh, it's all in a good cause, of course, and he says he enjoys having a hammer in his hand sometimes.'

I think I missed something, Cassidy thought. This isn't making sense.

Her confusion must have showed in her eyes, because Jenna said, 'It's his men's group again. Today they're re-roofing a house over on Charlotte Street for a family who can't afford to have the work done.'

Cassidy couldn't have been any more startled if someone had stuck a pin in her favourite red balloon. 'But——'

'Reid's heart has always been easily touched when there are children involved,' Jenna said.

As I have every reason to know, Cassidy thought. She felt a little as if she were suffocating.

'And this family—I am sorry, Cassidy; it was thoughtless of me, to bring the subject up. I don't wish to upset you,' Jenna said. 'But I've never had the opportunity before to tell you that I was sorry about your baby.'

Your baby—as if it hadn't also been her grandchild. All the bitterness Cassidy had ever felt towards Jenna Cavanaugh flooded back into her heart, and she said, crisply, before she had a chance to consider whether it was wise, 'That is some comfort, of course. I wonder if you would have said the same thing if he had lived.'

'The baby? Or Kent?' Jenna didn't wait for an answer. 'You're very angry, I see. Reid told me you were, but I thought surely by now——'

Cassidy set her cup and saucer down with a little crash. 'You thought what? That I'd have realised my proper place? Am I supposed to thank you for not allowing Kent to marry me?'

'Kent was of age,' Jenna said quietly. 'I had nothing to say about what he did.'

'Well, he didn't see it that way. He told me you absolutely refused to meet me, to even consider the possibility——'

Jenna leaned forward. Her jaw was taut, her mouth a thin line. 'Don't you understand, Cassidy? He was my son, and he's dead; I don't want to speak badly of him.' There were tears in her eyes.

But Cassidy had gone too far to stop there. 'Why wouldn't you even give us a chance?'

'But he didn't tell me about you, Cassidy. He—Kent lied to you when he said he had.'

'I don't believe you. Give me one reason why he would have done that!'

Jenna stood up, slowly. 'Because he was Kent,' she said, very quietly. 'I'm sorry, Cassidy—this is not the conversation I hoped that we would have. Perhaps another time.'

Don't bet on it, Cassidy thought bitterly. But she obediently rose to her feet and watched as Jenna gathered up the coffee things. I must have been imagining that comfortable old lady I thought I saw in her at first, she thought. This is the aristocrat; there's no doubt about that.

She drove slowly down Charlotte Street, not really caring whether she saw a roofing crew at work or not, unsure whether—if she did see Reid—she would even stop. But when she spotted a half-dozen men on the roof of a dilapidated two-and-a-half-storey house, her heart rose into her throat, and before she knew what she was doing she had parked her car across the street and was standing at the foot of the ladder, her neck craned so she could look up at them.

Reid was sitting at the very peak, stripped to the waist as if he were on a beach, doing nothing—he must be waiting for supplies, she thought. He called down, 'Did you hunt me up so you could take me out for lunch?'

'Not exactly.'

'That's a shame.'

'What do you think you're doing up there, anyway, Cavanaugh?'

He shrugged. 'Getting a suntan.'

'Skin cancer, more likely. Put your shirt on!'

'Bring it up, and I will.'

She looked at the pitch of the roof and shuddered.

A young woman who was arranging food on a picnic table near the front porch said, 'I don't blame you. My husband's up there with yours, learning how to do this. I finally just stopped looking.'

Cassidy felt compelled to correct her. 'He's not my husband. But still, when I see him up there——'

Someone carried a bundle of shingles up to Reid, and the rhythmic bang of his hammer began to echo off the houses across the street.

'It's your house?' Cassidy asked.

The young woman nodded and continued to unwrap cold cuts and set out bowls of potato salad. A small girl peered out from behind her mother, one finger in her mouth.

'Then can I help, at least?' Cassidy asked practically, reaching for a package of ham. 'You're right—I'd better not watch. I'm getting dizzy as it is.'

By the time the first slope of the roof was completed, Cassidy was on the best of terms with the young woman, but despite her best efforts the child still remained shy. So when the little girl burst away from her mother and went running across the lawn, Cassidy was startled, until she turned to see Reid, once more safely on the ground, scooping the child up in his arms.

The young woman handed her a plate.

Cassidy looked at it and protested, 'Angela, I just need to talk to Reid for a minute. I didn't barge in on your party so you could feed me!'

The woman shrugged. 'You may need all the stamina you can get.'

Something in her tone made Cassidy turn around to look, and when she saw Reid climbing to the roof again, with the little girl in front of him on the ladder, eagerly grasping at the next rung, she wheeled back to face Angela. 'You're letting him take that child up there?'

Angela shrugged. 'Don't be fooled by the way my daughter the tomboy has been acting in the last half-hour. They hauled her off that ladder a dozen times this morning, and she only stayed on the ground when Reid promised he'd take her up to see it at lunchtime.'

'That shy baby? You're right,' Cassidy said faintly. 'Stamina——'

But the two adventurers reached the ground safely again, and Reid brought his plate over under the spreading oak tree where Cassidy was thoughtfully drinking a can of pop. She moved, a little, and he sat down beside her with his back propped against the trunk of the tree. He'd put his shirt on again, though he hadn't bothered to button it, and the solar heat his body had absorbed on the roof seemed to radiate. He was too hungry, and Cassidy too preoccupied, for conversation.

She was thinking about his mother. Kent had lied to her, Jenna had said, *because he was Kent*. She had acted as if the admission were being twisted from her on the torture rack. But what on earth had the woman meant?

The child appeared beside Reid with a slice of coconut layer cake on a paper plate. She plopped down next to him and, with her mouth full, asked, 'This cake is delicious. Will you take me up again this afternoon?'

Reid eyed the plate. 'If you'll go and get me a slice of that cake, yes.'

The child obediently put down her plate and trotted off towards the picnic table.

'That was bribery,' Cassidy mused. 'And you gave in.'

Reid shrugged. 'I can't help it. Are all women born with this bloodthirsty instinct when it comes to negotiating? She's only five years old; she can't have learned it in school.'

'It's a good thing for you that your labour unions are all headed by men. I thought that's what you were doing today, by the way.' She kept her voice carefully casual.

'I'm disappointed. I thought you missed me so much that you came looking for me, and now I find it was only business.' He ate his cake, accompanied by the cheerful chatter of the child, and stretched out on the lawn for a few minutes' rest.

Cassidy didn't mind the silence. She pulled her knees up to her chin and wrapped her arms around them, and sat there quietly, too absorbed in her own thoughts to notice the banter of the rest of the group of volunteers.

Because he was Kent...

She closed her eyes and tried to imagine Kent sitting atop that roof on a warm spring day, nailing on shingles, just for the pleasure of helping out a young family who had suffered misfortune and unemployment. Kent, shepherding that child safely up the ladder to see the view, and volunteering to do it again. Kent——

Kent would never have married me, she thought. He was quite willing to play house, to have the convenience and the fun—but he didn't want the responsibility. If I'd had a chance to tell him about the baby, he'd have said that it was my problem. Jenna was telling the truth. Kent never mentioned me to her; her opposition to our marriage was nothing but a fairy-tale, a convenient fiction that he made up to keep me from pressuring him.

It was not a sudden, blinding revelation, but a tired, sad admission. Somewhere, she realised, in a dark corner of her mind, the knowledge had been lurking for a long time, too painful—too evil—to be faced and rooted out. But she had known.

She sat there for a long time, and when the men went back to work she got up and helped Angela deal with the mess, and then they set tomato plants out in the little spaded-up garden spot at the back of the house. By mid-afternoon the roof was done, and this time she could actually smile and wave when Reid and the little girl called down to them from the top of the ladder.

Afterwards, Reid wandered around to the back of the house and watched as the roots of the last tomato seedling were firmly packed in the black earth. 'I hope you're waiting around to give me a ride home, Cassidy,' he said. 'The other guys went on without me.'

She shrugged and got up and went to wash her hands. As they drove away, she looked in the mirror and saw Angela and her husband and little girl standing in the edge of the street, necks craned to proudly inspect the new roof.

'You're very quiet,' Reid said. 'Did something fall apart, and you didn't want to tell me with a lot of people around?'

'No. It's just——' She didn't want to meet his eyes, but her gaze drifted to him anyway. 'I feel sorry for them. Angela told me they were doing so well at first, but now he's been without work for months, and they've hardly been able to hold on to the house at all.' He didn't answer, and Cassidy went on almost fiercely, 'She told me that if it weren't for this group of yours they'd have given up by now. When your mother told me about your men's club——'

'So that's how you found me.'

She ignored him. 'My first thought was some kind of stag organisation with girls jumping out of cakes——'

He grinned. 'That's cute, Cassidy.'

'And then to find out it's a charity thing, instead——' She swallowed hard. 'That's why you're doing it, isn't it? The whole new company, I mean. The whole new approach to building homes—it's for people like Angela and her husband. Not only to live in, but to work at building——'

'I'd like to hire him, yes,' Reid said mildly. 'But he isn't trained.'

'And that's what you're going to do, isn't it? Hire people and train them and move them up as soon as they're skilled enough——'

'Do you have to make it sound like a crime?' Reid asked plaintively. 'Want to come in for a drink?'

She was a little startled to find herself in front of the Cottage; she hadn't given a thought to the twists and turns of the streets, and yet she had driven straight to it.

She stared straight ahead for a moment, and said, 'Yes. I have an apology to make to your mother.'

Reid's eyebrows arched. 'About the men's club?'

'No,' Cassidy said stiffly. 'Something else.'

'Well, I'm sorry, but she isn't here. She and Mrs Miller left this afternoon for the summer house to get it opened up and cleaned.'

'Summer house? You never used to have——'

'I bought it a couple of years ago. Mother finds it difficult to cope with the heat here, so I bought a place down on Table Rock Lake. She always spends most of the summer there. Do you still want your drink, or shall we sit here in the car and broil for a while longer?'

'Oh. Of course.'

The inside of the Cottage was dim and quiet and inviting. The instant he felt the cool air, Reid sighed; Cassidy didn't know if he was even aware he had. 'You look as if you're dying for a shower,' she said.

He hesitated, but only for a moment. 'You'll wait? Can you really stay away from the sorority house for a whole afternoon, and have time for a drink, too?'

She thought about throwing a shoe at him, but finally she answered seriously instead. 'My assistant is also the cook, so she's spending the day in the kitchen anyway, and I'm taking the night watch.'

'Oh, yes. The dance,' he said flatly, and headed down the hall.

'Dancing is a lot more fun than making fifty dozen hors-d'oeuvres,' Cassidy called after him.

The refrigerator was full of fruit and there was an electric juicer nearby, so she entertained herself while he was gone by creating two tall glasses of icy orange juice. She was just adding a bit of lemon for zest when Reid returned, reached over her shoulder to pick up a glass, and drained it in three swallows. 'That wasn't bad,' he said.

'How would you know?' She glared at him. 'That was gourmet orange juice. It was meant to be sipped and savoured.' She picked up her own glass. 'Like this.'

He observed, obediently. It made her nervous, and when a fragment of orange pulp clung to the corner of her mouth she tried to capture it discreetly with the tip of her tongue. Reid watched intently for a moment and then took the glass out of her hand and set it aside. 'All right. You've sipped enough. I'll savour.' His arms went around her with swift sureness.

'That's not what I——'

But he obviously wasn't listening. With lingering tenderness he kissed the evidence of her orange juice away, his tongue gently caressing the corner of her mouth before moving on to the hollow of her cheek and then to the sensitive spot just in front of her ear.

What was that nonsense she'd been telling herself? she thought hazily. Something about how the crazy physical reaction she'd had to his kiss was nothing personal at all, just an automatic, reflexive response. Well, it had been nonsense, all right, because this was personal. It was *very* personal...

She fitted neatly into his arms, with her face tilted up to his, and her hands crept up to caress his hair, still damp and cool after his shower. His mouth met hers, squarely, and lingered there for a very long time, and then he said, softly, 'What were you saying, Cassidy?'

'Nothing.' It was not much more than a croak.

He smiled, a little, and drew her closer yet, his hands spread firmly across the small of her back. But the pressure wasn't necessary to hold her close against him; nothing, she thought, save his own action, could pull her away just now. A moment later his fingers wandered upwards under her pullover blouse and released the catch on her bra.

She gasped, just a little, and stiffened in his arms.

'What's wrong?' he whispered, against her mouth.

Reluctantly, she said, 'This—it's getting out of hand.'

'No, it's not.' His breath was coming unsteadily, and his fingertips slipped surely over her ribs and stroked the soft secret skin of her breasts. 'This is exactly what I intended to happen.' His thumbs found the delicate peaks, and she shivered as darts of pleasure struck straight to the core of her body.

'But just a few days ago—— You said you wouldn't take advantage of me——'

'I wanted to make love to you that night, Cassidy. But you were emotionally overwrought and out of control, and there were thirty-two girls who might have knocked on the door at any moment. Now, here, there are only the two of us, and we certainly know what we're doing.'

She gulped.

'I'm not a saint,' he went on, 'and I made up my mind that night that if you ever gave me that sort of invitation again—when you weren't upset and confused about the difference between comfort and desire—that I would not walk away. It seems to me this is that invitation. So tell me, Cassidy—am I taking advantage of you? Or am I just doing what you want?'

His mouth came down on hers again, almost demanding this time. If his previous kisses had been fire, this was explosion; every bone in her body seemed to shatter under the force of it, leaving her limp and weak in his arms and unable to deny the frantic hunger that he had fanned to life inside her.

It was the only answer he seemed to need—it was certainly the only one Cassidy was capable of giving him—and his touch grew instantly gentle again as he

guided her down the long hall and into the one room of
his house where she had never gone before.

He did plan this, she thought a little hazily, for the
bed was already turned down. Or had Mrs Miller done
that before she left? She had done it each night, for
Cassidy, but . . .

Then Reid kissed her again, and Cassidy stopped
thinking of anything but him, and how he could make
her feel.

He was a patient lover—incredibly so, she thought,
for she could sense the tension in him, and the way he
suppressed his own needs in order to fan her passion to
white heat. He seemed to know instinctively how to touch
her in order to send her into spasms of mindless delight,
but that was nothing in comparison with the way she
felt when finally they were one. The sensations they
shared then were an aching, shimmering joy which
rubbed each nerve with sandpaper until she couldn't
stand it any more. And so she screamed his name and
clung to him, while the world spun crazily out of their
control.

It took a long time to recover even the minimal power
of movement, but finally she was able to let her hands
roam once more with gentleness to stroke his hair, his
skin. And finally her senses began to settle back to
normal——

No, not to normal, she reflected, and wondered,
without the slightest concern, whether she would ever
again feel normal. And she thought, How could I have
made myself believe that I never wanted to share my life
with a man again?

But not just any man would do, whispered the still
small voice of her conscience. Not just any man at all.

The impact of this sudden understanding was as stunning as if it had been pounded into her skull with a mallet.

She had not found another man to share her life, because there was none who measured up. Reid had been right in his assessment of that question. But it had not been her loyalty to Kent which had kept her from finding another man; it was not Kent she had used as her standard of measurement. Even then—four years ago—it had been Reid.

She had fallen in love with Reid, and it was the knowledge that there was no one who could take his place which had prevented her from even looking.

CHAPTER EIGHT

THE knowledge settled into Cassidy's heart with ease, as if it were the missing piece of a jigsaw puzzle—the key piece which made everything else fall neatly into place. It explained why she had been so afraid to meet Reid again, and also why, when a couple of days went by without a sight of him, she began to grow restless and discontented. It accounted for the frustration and anger and the fear she felt, and also that odd peacefulness that crept over her sometimes when she was with him. And most of all, it explained precisely why she had been so unwilling to stay and face him, after the miscarriage four years ago. All her reasons had been honest ones, but underneath had been a hidden motive, so deeply buried that she had not even known it was there.

I hid from him, she admitted to herself, because I was afraid to know what he would do. I wasn't afraid that he would be angry with me for leaving; I was terrified that he *wouldn't* be. I was afraid that he wouldn't try to convince me to take the money; I was afraid that he really didn't give a damn what happened to me. And so I hid from him because I didn't want him to tell me to go, and I dreaded having to face the fact that he didn't want me to stay. I hid because I wanted to pretend with every day that passed that he was looking for me, that he wanted me back—that I mattered to him, after all ...

And where did that leave her now? He had made love to her a few minutes ago as if he were starving for her warmth, but what did that mean? It certainly implied some lasting value—but he had also said that he had planned this episode, that he had cold-bloodedly decided not to turn down such an enticing invitation if she offered it again...

Don't ask too many questions, she told herself. Take the pleasure of the moment, and do not ask for more.

He kissed the tender hollow at the base of her throat, and smiled down into her eyes, and gently freed himself.

The party's over, she thought. She sat up, hugging her knees, not looking at him, though she knew he was watching her. 'The dance,' she said suddenly. 'I have to go back.' She craned her neck to see the face of the alarm clock on the bedside table.

'I was afraid you'd remember that.' But his tone was calm, matter-of-fact, as if it really didn't concern him. He fluffed his pillow and propped it and himself up against the tall carved headboard. The tip of his index finger ran gently up the length of her spine, sending random little sparks out through her body like the misfiring of a badly out-of-tune engine. His hand formed a cup at the base of her neck and began to massage the tenseness away, stroking each muscle separately. 'But you don't have to go just yet. There's a little time.'

She almost asked if he would come to the dance after all. The question trembled on the tip of her tongue, and then she firmly put it aside. Obviously he had not forgotten the dance; had that, too, been a part of his plan when he had invited her into his bed? It might have struck him as the perfect way to make certain she didn't overstay her welcome. It was Saturday night, after all; he might even have a date. If he *was* going to be married, it would be only reasonable if he did——

Until that moment she had put out of her mind Jenna's remarks about two women sharing a house; the truth was, Cassidy admitted, that she had not wanted to remember what Jenna had said, because she had not wanted to think of another woman in his life. But once the memory returned it was a full-blown agony, absorbing every other thought in her mind.

'I have to go now,' she said in a quick, choked voice, and his hand dropped away from her shoulder-blade. He did not move or protest as she retrieved her clothes from the scattered heap on the carpet, but once she was dressed he stopped her at the bedroom door.

He kissed her long and lingeringly, as if, she thought despairingly, it was the last time. She leaned against the door and looked up at him for a long moment and thought, Even if this is the end of it, I do not regret an instant of what we shared. She stood on her tiptoes and kissed his cheek and whispered, 'Thank you, Reid.' Then she ducked out of the room and was down the hall to the front door and out to her car before there was time for an answer.

'You're doing it again,' she accused herself as she drove, a bit shakily, back towards the sorority house. 'You ran away so you can tell yourself that he would have said all sorts of wonderful things, if only he'd had the opportunity. You're a fool, Cassidy Adams. You can't allow it to matter to you—whether or not he's thinking of getting married again——'

Though, when she thought about it, *getting married again* didn't seem to be quite the right way to phrase it; after all, he hadn't been married to Cassidy at all, in any real sense——

And how I wish he had been, she thought.

The level of confusion in the sorority house had risen to an all-time peak. Between the final frantic efforts of the decorating committee to finish off the scenery in the ballroom, and the frenzied bustle on the second floor as the twenty-five girls who weren't still decorating tried to fit themselves into the bathrooms all at once, Cassidy was almost dazed within minutes. She poked her head into the kitchen, where trays of food lined every flat surface and were stacked three high on the tables. The cook looked fierce, and Cassidy didn't have the heart to ask how things were going; she was afraid that a tray of hors-d'oeuvres might come flying across the room at her.

She checked out the dining-room, where the buffet table was already set up with serving dishes in place, ready to be filled from the kitchen supplies by the wait-resses hired for the evening, made sure the most valuable of the lamps and vases in the parlours were safely out of harm's way, and went upstairs to get dressed herself.

Her own tiny apartment was an island of peace, though not of quiet; the girls' excitement had banished that commodity from the entire house. Cassidy took a brief shower, grumbling, as she stood under the icy spray, 'I should have known that the hot-water supply couldn't hold out under these conditions!'

She brushed her hair more vigorously than usual in an effort to get her blood circulating again, but she was still shivering by the time she was dressed. That problem would soon be remedied, she told herself. Put a hundred people or so in that third-floor ballroom, without air-conditioning, on a warmer than usual evening in May, and there would be no trouble at all. She would probably be grateful, before the evening was out, that her dress was sleeveless and cut low in the back.

She was running late, and by the time she climbed the stairs to the third floor the band was already warming up and the room seemed absurdly full of people. But perhaps it was only the girls' dresses that made it seem so crowded; one brushed past her in a hoop skirt, and another was sporting a taffeta bow that was as big as a bustle.

Cassidy's own dress was absurdly simple in comparison. It was ivory jersey, draped in an almost-Grecian style and falling in soft folds to her toes. The only ornament was the gold filigree that encircled the high waistline and formed a clasp just below her breasts. But then, she told herself, as a chaperon, she was supposed to fade into the background, not be a star.

The band started to play, and the first couples went out on to the floor. Heather, looking lovely despite the marathon session to finish the ballroom, winked at Cassidy over her partner's shoulder, and when they drifted past the girl murmured, 'Don't worry, Mom— we can chaperon ourselves.' She tilted her head towards the far end of the room and smiled. 'Have fun. We all certainly intend to.'

Cassidy frowned in puzzlement. Then the crowd on the dance-floor shifted in a new mosaic, and in the dim light, between the blurs of pastel dresses, she saw a tall man in faultless black evening clothes slowly working his way between the dancers.

Her heart climbed into her throat and stuck there as she stared at him, and Reid came straight to her. 'Don't tell me,' he murmured. 'The way you're looking at me, I must have put my tie on upside-down.'

She shook her head.

'Then may I have the honour?' he asked.

She didn't know about the soft little sigh she gave as they began to join the rhythm of the music, as if every drop of tension in her was draining away. But he looked down at her with a half-smile and held her even more closely.

She had never danced with him before. But if I had, she thought, I would have known what a wonderful lover he would be. His touch was firm, but not confining; this was obviously a man who was sure of himself and at ease with the world, a man who had nothing to prove, so he could relax.

'You are the most beautiful woman here,' he murmured into her ear.

She shook her head. 'Unless you mean I'm the only woman.'

That seemed to amuse him. 'And the rest are mere girls? That's true enough.'

The music shifted to a slow and gentle love-song, and she put her head down on his shoulder and closed her eyes and let the scent of his soap remind her of all the things he had taught her earlier tonight.

And yet she sensed that there was a great deal more to know, and if he wanted to teach her she would be more than willing to learn...

She had no idea how long they danced; she knew the tempo changed often and the songs flowed one after another. She could have gone on forever, and when Reid spoke and broke the enchanted mood she was almost resentful.

'I can't believe any city inspector approved this kind of crowd,' he said, and the bantering tone was completely gone from his voice.

'The fire inspector was here yesterday—I know that. I didn't talk to him, but that's why there are no candles. The girls were furious.' Cassidy opened her eyes, reluctantly. The ballroom seemed to have become a seething mass of humanity while she wasn't looking. She had seen the guest list, but it didn't seem possible that it could have produced so many people.

Reid looked a bit dissatisfied, but he didn't pursue the subject. The tempo shifted again, speeding up to a frenzied pace with the dancers clapping their hands to the beat. Reid said mildly, 'This isn't my style. How about a breath of fresh air?'

Cassidy nodded. 'It is stuffy in here. And there's food downstairs, too. I didn't have dinner——'

Reid grinned, and she turned very pink and picked up her skirt and hurried through the crowd to the twisting stairway.

He caught up with her at the foot of the main staircase and drew her back into a secluded nook in the shadow of the banister. 'I wasn't thinking of snacks, actually,' he murmured, 'but of a quiet, lonely little corner where I could do this——'

The music seemed to follow them, the heavy beat almost vibrating as if to remind Cassidy of her duties. 'I am the chaperon,' she pointed out, regretfully. 'I can't be caught kissing on the stairs.'

Reid sighed. 'All right, then—I'll settle for food. At least it's cooler down here.'

In the dining-room, the buffet table was lined with a mouth-watering display. Cassidy picked up a pinwheel sandwich from the nearest tray. 'I love these things,' she said. 'The filling is liverwurst and cream cheese, and it's my absolute favourite.' She popped it whole into her mouth and said, 'Is it my imagination, or is the air sort of strange-looking in here?'

'If you think this is bad, you should see the kitchen,' volunteered the waitress who was refilling trays.

Cassidy's eyes were stinging. She rubbed at them absent-mindedly, and suddenly, to her horror, things began to add up. 'It's smoke!' she whispered. 'Oh, Reid, all those innocent kids upstairs——'

He was staring at the ceiling. 'It's not smoke. It's dust.' He pointed up at a carved wooden beam. '"All those innocent kids upstairs", as you put it, are bouncing around and shaking the plaster loose.'

She released a long breath of relief. 'For a moment there, I thought——'

'And in a house of this age, and this style of construction, that simply shouldn't be happening,' Reid said, almost to himself. He turned to the waitress. 'You said the kitchen is worse?'

She nodded.

A particularly loud blast of music from upstairs was accompanied by what sounded like a herd of buffalo crossing the ballroom floor. 'They're stomping their feet,' Cassidy said. 'It lets the band know they like the music——'

'Applauding was good enough in my day,' Reid said drily.

Cassidy pushed open the swinging doors to the kitchen and started inside. Reid's hand closed on her wrist and jerked her almost off her feet and back into the safety of the hallway, and together they watched as the kitchen ceiling collapsed.

A six-foot square section of plaster fell, as if in slow motion, and shattered into a billion fragments that splashed over appliances, floor, and food. Dust billowed up from the crash in a choking, boiling cloud.

Reid pushed Cassidy back and dived into the mess towards two waitresses who had been refilling trays almost directly under the fallen ceiling. A moment later the dust cleared a bit, and she saw him at the back door, propping it open, as the waitresses pushed past her into the hall.

'I'm getting out of here right now,' one of them said, shrilly. 'That does it. There's no food left to serve, anyway.'

Reid crossed the kitchen to open a window. 'That's the smartest idea I've heard in years,' he said crisply. The lock stuck, and he struggled with it. 'When was the last time this thing was opened, anyway?'

'When the ventilating system was put in, I suppose.'

The lock broke loose and came off in his hand. He stared at it for a long moment, with a stunned expression on his face that almost made her want to laugh, and then he dug a penknife out of his pocket and started to poke at the wooden frame. It crumbled under his touch.

She had never seen anyone look so grim. Her desire to giggle faded into nothingness.

'Where's the cellar door?' he snapped.

'There.' Cassidy pointed to the corner of the kitchen. 'Reid, what——?'

He said, over his shoulder, 'I suspect you've got the worst case of termites I've ever seen. Get every one of those kids out of the house. Right now.'

'And how do you suggest I do that?'

'I don't care, Cassidy. Just get it done before they decide to start stomping their feet again, or this whole house will end up as a pile of toothpicks, and instead of writing the lead story in Monday's *Alternative* you'll be part of it!'

It was a very subdued group of girls who sat on the front lawn in the wee hours of the morning, their finery wet with dew and the night air chilly against their bare arms and backs. They were huddled together under blankets loaned by the sorority next door. None of them had so much as a shawl of her own.

The guests were gone, and most of the Alphas were already settled for the night in the neighbouring house, where they had bedded down on the living-room floor. Only the members of the governing council remained on the lawn, staring up in disbelief at the big old house, which loomed in the moonlight as big—and seemingly as solid—as ever.

It was hard to believe that it was not. But the city building inspector that Reid had roused from sleep to survey the damage had just told them that their house could not be occupied again without major reconstruction.

'I don't understand,' Heather said, finally. 'How can such a tiny little insect eat up a whole house?'

Reid moved a little on the cold concrete bench where he sat next to Cassidy. 'For one thing, no one seems to know when the place was last inspected for termites; they may have been chomping away at the support beams in the cellar for a year or more. And if you're wondering why it happened tonight—well, you had twice the number of people in that ballroom that it was intended to hold.'

Heather's gaze dropped to the grass at her feet.

'The extra weight on the framework was more than the house could stand in its weakened condition, so it started twisting.'

'What about our clothes and books and stuff?' one of the other girls asked. 'Do we have to just leave it all there?'

The inspector shook his head. 'I think we'll find, on closer inspection, that if a few people go in at a time and move cautiously there should be no danger. It was the overload that caused the problem tonight; the house is badly damaged but, thanks to Mr Cavanaugh, it's no longer in danger of immediate collapse.'

'What a *comfort*,' Heather sighed. It was a master- piece of sarcasm.

Cassidy rose. 'Let's get you all settled for the night, now. There will be plenty of time to talk about it in the morning and decide what to do.' She shepherded them towards the house next door, where the elderly house- mother, in robe and night cream, was waiting to fuss over them.

'I wish I had a room to offer you, Cassidy,' she said worriedly. 'But unless you want to bunk with the girls on the floor, I'm afraid——'

'I'll look after her,' Reid said. 'Thanks for taking in the girls.' He drew Cassidy away.

'Reid, I don't even have a charge card, or a dime to my name,' she protested.

'Where do you think you'll need money?'

'My car keys are still up in my room, too——'

'I'll bring you back in the morning.'

'I really should stay with the girls, Reid.'

He ignored the protest and led her out to the Lincoln. It was a silent drive to Mission Hills; about halfway there, Cassidy started to shake uncontrollably, and by the time she was inside the house she was almost hysterical.

'I thought this might happen,' he said. He poured a shot of brandy for her from the bar in the family-room and sat down on the arm of the leather couch next to the chair where she huddled. 'The girls will be fine— most of them will never quite realise the danger they were in. But you and your overdeveloped sense of responsibility worry me.'

'I *am* responsible.' She drank the brandy, slowly. The violent shudders died down to an occasional shiver. 'I *was* responsible,' she added, quietly, and stopped there, not quite certain exactly what she meant.

He rubbed his eyes, and she realised for the first time how tired he must be. It was nearly four in the morning, and he had gone over every inch of that house with the inspector, while she had sat on the lawn. His hair was almost entirely grey at the moment, and his evening clothes were caked with plaster dust. 'Come on,' he said. 'Let's get you to bed.'

'Reid——' She hesitated, and looked up at him with doubt in her eyes.

'Look,' he said, and exasperation crept through his voice, 'after the night we've had, if I were to attack you right now it couldn't be called assault—it would be more like a miracle.'

She smiled a little, despite herself. 'I'm not exactly feeling passionate at the moment, either.'

'I'm not surprised. So do me a favour and come into my room for what's left of the night.'

Her eyebrows went up. 'Do *you* a favour?'

'Right. That way if you have nightmares, I won't have to get out of bed in order to stop you from jumping out of a window.' He yawned, enormously, and started down the hall towards his bedroom as if he didn't care whether she followed.

There was some logic to his reasoning. And she had to admit, a few minutes later, as she lay beside him and listened to the quiet pattern of his breathing, that it was awfully nice to be there, so close to his solid warmth, knowing that nothing was going to harm her. She turned over on her side and nestled against him and slept.

She didn't have nightmares, unless waking to find herself alone, with full sunshine cascading across the coverlet, was to be considered a bad dream. And even that dissipated a moment later when Reid came in with a bed tray. On it were two mugs and a basket, and the aroma made Cassidy sit straight up. 'Are those blueberry muffins?' she asked eagerly.

He nodded. 'Mrs Miller made them; she always feels guilty when she leaves me to fend for myself. But that answers my first question—you obviously feel much better this morning.' He set the tray down. 'And you're looking very good, too.'

She realised, abruptly, that neither of them had bothered to find her a nightgown, and she pulled the sheet up to her nose, embarrassed not because of her display but because he might think she was trying to entice him.

But Reid laughed and sat down on the edge of the bed. He wasn't much better off for clothes at the moment himself; his tartan bathrobe showed almost as much chest as he'd displayed yesterday on the roof when he hadn't been wearing any shirt at all.

She readjusted the sheet, holding it firmly tucked under her arms, and reached eagerly for a muffin at the same instant that Reid did. The muffin forgotten, he caught her hand and held it up, looking at the bruise which circled her entire wrist. His face tensed, and he traced the dark shadow with a gentle fingertip. 'I'm sorry about this.'

'For heaven's sake, Reid, don't be silly. You saved me a nasty bump on the head.'

'And then I sent you upstairs into something that could have been a great deal worse,' he said quietly. 'Cassidy, it was the only thing I could do—sending you into danger to get those kids out.'

Her breath caught, as if there were a rough spot in her throat. 'While you went to the cellar to try to prop things up,' she said. 'And everything would have landed on top of you, if——' She couldn't finish the sentence, couldn't even bring herself to think of the possibility. Those year-long moments while she had been almost pushing kids down the stairs, down the fire escapes, while the house seemed to tremble and shudder under her— and the long minutes, later, when everyone had been out except Reid, and it seemed that he was never going to appear...

For a space that seemed like eternity, but probably was only a minute or two, they looked at each other. Then Reid set the tray carefully on to the floor and reached for her. His eyes had gone so dark that she could scarcely tell where pupil and iris met, and the way his kiss burned against her skin made her ache with gladness that she was in his arms again.

He tugged the sheet away, and bent his head to take the eager tip of her breast between his teeth. The mere touch was like lighting a fuse. She moaned a little and pushed at his robe, eager to be rid of even the flimsiest barricade that kept them apart.

He kissed the hollow between her breasts, and his fingertips explored the most sensitive, secret cells of her body. She writhed against him, wordlessly pleading, and he whispered, 'Not yet. There are a good many things I intend to do to you first, Cassidy, until neither of us can stand any more.'

It became almost a battle, with Reid finding way after way to bring her pleasure, and Cassidy striving to undermine the self-control that allowed him to go on. She won, ultimately, of course, but by then it no longer mattered—the only thing she cared about was the almost surrealistic ecstasy of his possession, and the knowledge that in this way, at least, he was hers. In this way, at least, he loved her, too.

For there was not the least glimmer of doubt that it was love she felt for him. And not just physical love, either, though heaven knew she found such joy in the joining of their bodies that it could, if she allowed it to do so, overshadow other considerations.

She wanted to cherish him, to comfort him, to share with him all the joys and sorrows that life could throw at them, for as long as the world went on.

And if he did not want to share those things with her—what then? What if it was only physical love that he wished to share with her? What if it was only for right now, and soon he would want to be free?

But there was no choice, really. To tear herself apart from him now, to rob herself of the memories she could have, no matter what happened, would be as much suicide as taking a knife to her wrists. She loved him with her mind, with her heart, with her body, and that would never stop, no matter what happened to the two of them.

The coffee grew stone-cold, and much later, after the world had stopped rocking on its axis, Reid got up and made another pot. They drank it, and polished off the blueberry muffins, in the breakfast-room.

It was safer that way, Reid said, because she did have to go back to the house some time.

Cassidy turned a little pink at the implication that if it was left up to her she'd never get out of bed again, and said, 'I'm going to resign.'

Reid stopped chewing his muffin and stared at her as if she'd suddenly turned into the serpent in the Garden of Eden.

Oh, hell, she thought. Now he thinks I'm angling to stay here, that I've interpreted this single night as an invitation to permanence.

'I'll have to see them through this,' she said quickly. 'But as soon as I can reasonably resign—well, I just don't think I can handle this sort of pressure any longer. It's a much harder job than I thought.' You're babbling, she told herself. 'So I'll have to reconsider my finances, too— I'll keep on paying you back, of course, but it will take longer, and——'

'Dammit, Cassidy!'

'You promised,' she said unsteadily. Her hands clenched on her cup so tightly that she thought it might shatter under the pressure. She looked up at him through tear-misted eyes. 'You promised not to say anything more about the money.'

He said something unprintable, under his breath, about promises. Then he pushed his chair back and began gathering up dirty dishes with a violent sort of efficiency. 'My mother has the guest bedroom,' he said, without looking at her. 'I think you'll find something there that you can adapt to wear.'

She was so grateful that he hadn't pursued the subject that she almost ran down the hall to the guest bedroom. Once it had been her room. It was here that Fudge had got his name, here that Reid had first kissed her... But there was no sense in thinking of things like that.

Rummaging through Jenna's wardrobe was an experience never to be forgotten. The woman was certainly no grandmotherly dumpling in pastel print house-dresses, that was for sure. Suits, evening gowns, lounging clothes, most with designer labels, all with that elusive quality called style... Finally she settled on a sporty true blue dress with ornamental top-stitching.

By the time she made up her mind, Reid had finished dressing; she found him in the family-room with the Sunday newspaper strewn out around his chair. He looked her up and down without comment.

'It's the newest look,' Cassidy said, pirouetting, determined to keep things light. 'I'm going to bring legs back into style—I didn't realise I was so much taller than your mother is.'

He didn't answer. 'Are you ready to go?'

'Almost. I have to get my dress from last night——'

'Leave it,' he said brusquely. 'You'll have enough to deal with today.'

She didn't argue. She certainly wasn't going to try to prolong this, when it was obvious he was ready to get rid of her.

Traffic was heavy around the sorority house. Sightseers, she thought, who had already heard about the near disaster. She stared from the car window herself as they crept up the street and stopped in front of the house next door.

Reid was staring straight ahead, as if still assessing the traffic. Cassidy allowed herself a long, lingering look at him.

Don't be silly, she told herself. It's not as if you'll never see him again.

But the annoying little voice at the back of her brain said, You may see him, that's true, but it will never be like this, again . . .

She swallowed hard. 'Thank you, Reid.' Her voice was a little rough. 'For everything.'

'I'll wait for you.'

'That's not necessary—I don't know how long I'll be, or——'

'I said I'll wait, Cassidy.'

A car horn honked behind them. Cassidy jumped; Reid didn't seem to hear it. Stubborn, she thought, but she couldn't quite bring herself to resent it; in fact, his insistence gave her sort of a warm little glow. 'Well, you can't wait here. You're blocking traffic.'

He smiled a little, at that. 'I'll be around behind the house. I want to see what the inspectors are finding this morning, anyway.'

She got out of the car without another word. The warm little glow inside her had died, with an almost audible pop.

He was deep in conversation with one of the city workers when she returned, and Cassidy sat on a bench in the back garden for a long while, waiting to be noticed. Finally, however, he came over. He put one foot up on the bench beside her and leaned an elbow on it. 'I got your car keys and your purse and some clothes.'

'You've been back in there? Reid——'

'How are the girls doing?'

She gave up; arguing with him had never been a good use of time, and it was too late to stop him, this time. 'They're fine—very grown-up and efficient about the whole thing. They'll just spread out among the other sorority houses for a while, and if this house can't be fixed by fall they'll rent something.'

He nodded. 'So which of the houses do you go to?'

'None of them. They don't need a house-mother for the present, so they very efficiently laid me off.' She smiled, with an effort. It was silly, she told herself, to be just a little hurt, when she'd already made up her mind to leave!

'Some gratitude,' he grumbled. 'Leaving you at a loose end after you saved their necks.'

'Don't take it personally, Reid,' she said crisply. But she ached a little, deep inside. Was he really saying that he wished she weren't at a loose end? She tried to be flippant. 'I don't suppose I can afford to buy a condo from you—would you happen to know of an apartment for rent?'

He didn't speak for a long time. 'Come stay with me,' he said softly.

She tried to laugh it off, instead. 'Reid, just because I'm a waif on the streets again, it doesn't mean you have to take me in. I have to stand on my own some time— find a place to live, and get on with my life.'

He reached out, as if to touch her cheek, but at the last moment his hand dropped away from her face. 'All right. But you can't do all that today. And until you can—come and stay with me, for a while.'

For a while—there were so many bitter-sweet implications to the phrase that she didn't even want to start thinking of them.

But did she honestly have a choice?

It wasn't her physical well-being that concerned her; she was not destitute, and there were apartments, hotels, rented rooms—she would not be homeless. It was her mental and emotional health she was thinking of now. Could she allow herself to take the risk of living with him—*for a while*? Of loving him, and investing herself in him, knowing all the time that it must soon end? If there was any hope of permanence, he would not have phrased the invitation as he had. Could she bear to inflict those wounds on herself?

But wouldn't it be even worse to turn her back, and walk away? Then she would have nothing at all, only the cold knowledge that she had, at all costs, protected herself. And it was already far too late for that. She had made that decision last night when she had torn down the protective wall that had surrounded her for so long and allowed him to make love to her. It was too late to start building it again.

He seemed to watch the conflict in her eyes, and to know when she reached her decision. He took her hand then, and eased her to her feet. 'Come home with me,' he said, and put his arm around her shoulders.

'For a while,' she whispered. It was all she could say.

CHAPTER NINE

FOR a while...

Every time the phrase danced through her mind, Cassidy deliberately turned her thoughts to other things, but as the days stole on she found it haunting her, echoing through her brain like the refrain of an old song—only half-remembered, but never quite forgotten either.

For a while... As far as she was concerned, days— weeks—years could quietly saunter by until she was eighty, and she would be feeling no impatience to be gone. But how long a while had Reid meant? Till their love-affair soured? Till his mother returned? Or only till Cassidy found a place to live and got on with her life?

Perhaps the details don't matter, she told herself. The one thing that's certain is that the end is coming; that was clear from the start. But when that undefined time is up and his patience is worn down—what then?

I must do something positive, she told herself more than once that week. I can't just wait around for him to tell me that he's tired of being a Good Samaritan; I ought at least to decide where I'll go and what I'll do. I ought to look for an apartment, think about furniture, figure out a budget...

And so she started each day by looking at the *Alternative*'s classified pages to see what was available. But there never seemed to be time to do anything else about it—to call the landlords, or to go and look at the apartments which were advertised. She found herself thinking sometimes that, even though she'd eliminated one job entirely, there still weren't enough hours in the day.

At least don't tell lies to yourself, Cassidy, she lectured on Wednesday morning, when the fresh edition lay open on her desk blotter with two possible apartments circled. She picked up her coffee-cup and cradled it between her hands, looking into the distance and seeing not the busy newsroom but the secret workings of her own mind.

If I don't go to look at apartments, she reflected, then I can't find one I like, so I can't possibly move, and I can continue to stay at the Cottage with Reid. And right now, she added—with the harsh insight that came from squarely facing an uncomfortable truth—I'd rather be thrown out bodily when he tires of me than to willingly give up one minute with him. I'd rather pretend than to have to face the reality that forever does not lie within my grasp. I don't want to remember that he's really only doing me a favour, and that I owe him the courtesy of not taking advantage of his generosity...

In the grey light of morning when she woke beside him and he smiled at her in that way that made her heart turn over, it was easy to forget that this was not reality. In the crisp freshness of evenings spent quietly together on the veranda, or in the busy patterns of the day when she found herself thinking of things she must remember to tell him, it hardly seemed possible that this was an instant clipped from time and not the way things would always be.

But sometimes she was forced to face the truth—that their talk of the future never included anything personal at all. When she had to admit that her world might end tomorrow—without warning and without recourse—the secret, essential, inner Cassidy simply wanted to curl up and die.

That was not the only thing, of course, that jolted her back to reality. There was the story, ever-present in both their minds. They spent a lot of time that week talking about all the possibilities, and he showed her not only the drawings but the tiny models that had been constructed to show the actual placement of the buildings on the hilly site and the varied looks of the finished units. He took her through some of the more elaborate condo complexes, too, and showed her the changes that could be made to lessen the costs without cutting the quality.

The story in her bottom desk drawer grew and lengthened as that infinite, loving detail made its way into the paragraphs. She didn't think he knew how far along it was; she wanted to surprise him when the whole thing was finally finished and he gave permission for its publication. And so she ignored his frown and still took notes of everything he said, though by now she hardly needed to write anything down. She understood it all, she thought, nearly as well as he did. And besides, there was something about his voice that made things sink into her brain and stick there, as indelibly as if they had been engraved...

Love, she told herself dispassionately. You've got quite a case, haven't you, Cassidy? The kind of illness for which there is no cure...

At the next desk, Chloe's computer terminal was flashing through a story screen by screen at a pace that would have made Cassidy dizzy. Then the screen blinked and went almost blank as the finished product was fed into the main computer terminal for storage. Chloe leaned back in her chair and stretched her arms above her head. 'The feeling of relief when it's done is incredible, isn't it?' she said. 'I've spent all week on that story, and it's wonderful to see it vanish from my life.'

'Don't you even keep a print-out for yourself?' Cassidy asked curiously.

Chloe shook her head. 'The computer hasn't ever eaten anything of mine.'

She sounded as if she thought it wouldn't dare, Cassidy mused. 'It's never destroyed any of my stuff, either, but I always make a hard copy for myself, just in case.'

'Of course, as slowly as you work, the chances would be increased,' Chloe said, so smoothly that Cassidy wasn't certain whether she had intended it to be an insult or if it had just turned out that way. 'I couldn't bear to spend weeks on one thing, without some variety.'

'I don't,' Cassidy said crisply.

'Well, you're certainly spending hours lost in thought about *something*, these days.' Chloe shrugged. 'Even Brian's beginning to notice that you're not up to your usual standard.'

'I don't think——' Cassidy stopped herself. She had found that there was no point in trying to respond to Chloe's catty remarks; it only made things worse. The woman had changed, and the situation had, too, and, though it was a blow to Cassidy to have her friend suddenly acting like this, she could see what had happened. The star reporter who had been so helpful to the new girl now saw that same new girl as competition, that was all. It was understandable. Given some time, things would get back to normal.

So Cassidy said calmly, 'I've got plenty to think about, don't you agree? Some of my things are still stranded in that condemned building, and until I find an apartment——'

Chloe's eyebrows went up, and Cassidy wanted to tear her own wayward tongue out by the roots. But before Chloe could comment, an almost tentative voice spoke from behind Cassidy's chair. 'I'm sorry to bother you at work——'

Cassidy spun around. 'Heather!' She was amazed at the rush of warmth she felt at the sight. It's probably just gratitude at being rescued from Chloe's curiosity, she told herself cynically. Still, it *was* nice to see the girl——

Heather put two Tyler-Royale shopping bags down beside Cassidy's desk. 'We finally got the last of the stuff out of the house,' she said. 'I had them take your rocking-chair and your bookcase over to the Sigma house till you can pick them up; is that all right? And there were a few of your things still lying around in odd places.' She gestured at the bags and grinned a little. 'I couldn't believe it—you were the one who was always telling us to keep our stuff picked up!'

Cassidy glanced at the bags, half expecting that Heather would have planted some luxurious lingerie on top, just to see the effect as she walked through the office. But the visible contents were innocuous enough. Her favourite teal-blue sweater was on top of one bag, and nestled next to it was the half-empty jar of olives Reid had sent her. It seemed an awfully long time ago.

'What about the house?' she asked.

Heather shuddered. 'They're starting work next week, and if all goes well——' She held up her hand, fingers crossed. 'The house will reopen in the fall. The girls are going to ask you to come back, you know.'

'That's nice——'

'No, it's not. It's self-preservation. It's been pretty horrible this week,' Heather confided. 'Being shuffled around during final exams is bad enough, but having to get used to all kinds of new house-mothers on top of it——'

'I don't believe it,' Cassidy teased. 'You can't mean that you actually learned to appreciate me!'

'Well, at least you can remember what it's like to be young. I swear that some of these people *never* were college age!'

Cassidy had to laugh; Heather was running true to form, after all.

Chloe was still looking thoughtful long after Heather was gone. 'I assumed you were still living with the girls, somewhere,' she said finally.

Cassidy had turned back to her computer terminal. She looked up, trying to hide her annoyance. 'No—they didn't need a house-mother any more.'

'Then where are you living?'

She sighed. Didn't Chloe ever give up? 'I've been staying with friends,' she said quietly.

'Darling, I had no idea!' Suddenly, Chloe was again the companion, the girlfriend, that Cassidy had cherished when she first came to work at the *Alternative*. 'I should have thought—you weren't paying rent at the house, were you? This must be a terrible shock to your budget, then, having to find a place for just a few months.'

'It's not easy.' Well, it wasn't really a lie, Cassidy told her conscience. It *wouldn't* be easy, if that were what she was doing. And surely she wasn't obliged to explain to Chloe, too, why she wasn't going back to the house when it was habitable again.

'Well, you must come to stay with us for part of the summer. Theresa would love it—she asked me just this morning why you hadn't been to see her lately.'

Cassidy's head was swimming. 'I'll —that's very generous of you, Chloe. But I couldn't put you to such a bother——'

'No bother,' Chloe mused. 'It will be just one big slumber party. Theresa will be so excited...'

And how, Cassidy wondered, am I supposed to get out of this, without embarrassing us all?

Reid was later than usual. Cassidy thought that she had quickly accustomed herself once more to his irregular hours, but as the clock ticked on and he didn't come she began to feel uneasy. When finally she heard the garage door open, she hurried to meet him, and scolded herself even as she did it.

You should be playing it cool, she lectured, and pretending not to notice when he gets home. It's his business, after all—and it's not wise of you to act possessive and nagging and suspicious, as if you had the right to question him about where he's been and why he's late!

But she met him at the back door anyway. He kissed her on the cheek, lightly.

The same way he probably kisses his mother, Cassidy thought. The uneasy feeling grew stronger.

He said, 'I'm starving. Let's just go out the way we are, and get a sandwich. Nothing fancy.'

She looked at him for a long moment. 'I'm making lasagne, Reid. It's almost ready—don't you smell it?' She thought the scent was wonderful, herself, a spicy aroma that wafted through the kitchen.

He sniffed the air. 'Oh—no, I hadn't. That's fine, then.'

But he didn't sound as if it was fine, and he picked at his meal as if he didn't recognise it. This is starving? she thought. He acts like a man who put away a seven-course meal two hours ago...

She couldn't help being annoyed; the lasagne was good—even better than she had hoped for. She'd gone to a lot of trouble this week trying to teach herself how to function in the kitchen. It just seemed better that way, she thought; she knew, from the well-stocked state of Mrs Miller's freezer, that Reid wouldn't have been eating out if he'd been alone, so it didn't seem fair to expect him to take her out for every meal, as he had unfailingly suggested.

And she was having some success, too. Cook books had never been her favourite form of reading material, but she was getting into the spirit of the thing, now, and he had really seemed to enjoy that rib roast last night. She'd even managed a pot of coffee this morning that he had approved. But now there was this——

It was a practically silent meal, and he didn't offer to help with the clean-up, as he had every other night. As she rinsed the plates and put them in the dishwasher she tried not to think about the implications of his silent preoccupation. It meant—it had to mean—that the time had come for her to go.

The remnants of the lasagne were really too caked-on for scrubbing; the only sensible thing to do was leave the pan to soak. Instead, she determinedly ran another sinkful of steaming sudsy water and began chipping off the baked-on cheese and noodles and sauce, as if her life and sanity depended on a spotless result. At least it was something to think about, to keep her from dwelling on what she must do next. For she could not go into the family-room to join him until she knew what she was going to say; she would not just wait for him to tell her that it was time. Better to bring it up herself than to wait for him to gently break the news to her. And it would be gentle, she was certain of that——

That was when the tears began to stream down her cheeks, burning a silent pathway.

It seemed only a moment later that Reid said, from the other side of the room, 'For heaven's sake, let that thing soak. That's why they make throw-away pans, you know—because it's senseless to spend all night scrubbing the reusable ones.'

He hadn't noticed her tears, she thought; he'd only come to the kitchen for another glass of iced tea or something. But if he was to see her like this——

Without considering the consequences, she raised her hands to her cheeks to wipe away the tears, and succeeded only in smearing detergent suds into her eyes, down her face, and around her mouth. It was the final blow, and she began to sob in earnest.

Reid said, more gently, 'Mrs Miller isn't going to beat you for ruining the damned pan, you know. I'll buy her another one and she'll never know the difference——' Then he stopped, abruptly, and those grey eyes seemed to zero in on her trembling mouth. 'That isn't why you're crying, is it?'

She shook her head. Suds dripped from her chin and down the front of her sweater.

He mopped her face with the tea towel and took hold of her chin, raising it till she had to look at him. 'What is it, Cassidy?' he asked softly, and the tone of his voice made her want to cry all the more.

Instead, she gulped and fixed her gaze on the second button of his shirt and thought, It's better to do it myself than to wait. At least that way I'll have the shreds of my pride left, and that's better than having nothing at all...

'I'm leaving,' she said. Her voice was almost hoarse. 'I—I have to go—now. It's time, Reid.'

He didn't say anything at all, just looked at her long and steadily. And suspiciously, she thought.

She tried to smile, to reassure him. 'You know it; I know it. So why drag it out?'

His fingertip lifted to her cheek and traced the path a tear had taken. 'You're not very happy about it.'

'Of course not. But I can see what's coming, Reid—can't you? I'm beginning to feel tied down; so are you, if you're honest.'

He sighed a little, but he didn't deny it.

'Before long, we'd be resenting each other, and I—I don't want that——' Damn, she thought. A little more and I'll be crying again. She swallowed hard and tried again. 'You don't want that to happen, either—do you?'

'No,' he said quietly. 'No, I don't.'

It was very difficult, standing there by the kitchen sink, so close to him that she could almost feel each breath he took—though, if she was honest, she had to admit that he had that effect on her from any distance.

The towel that he had used to dry her face still dangled from his hand, as if he had forgotten it entirely. She tugged it out of his grip and wiped her hands, drying each finger as carefully as if she were about to do surgery. It helped a little to give her attention to such everyday things.

'There's no need for you to go,' he said, a little gruffly.

For an instant, hope leaped to life in her heart. Did he mean—*could* he mean——?

'Not tonight, at any rate,' he said. 'It's probably just as well—I ought to be over at the Kendrick Hotel right now, anyway. I was going to wait till morning to go, but——'

She was staring at the towel, still clutched between her hands. It was trembling like an aspen leaf, and her knuckles were white.

'The union people finally got their act pulled together,' Reid went on, as casually as if it didn't matter at all. 'The last of them will be arriving in the morning, and we'll be closeted there at the hotel till it's settled—one way or the other.'

The announcement stunned her for a moment. What a fool you are, she wanted to scream at herself. The conference, the condos, the story—she had been focusing so closely on her own concerns, her own feelings, that she had not even remembered any of that. So that was why he had been so preoccupied! Now that she knew, she could see the tension in him, and the stress that was building as this confrontation neared. She could see it all, now that it was too late to take back what she had said, and too late to extract herself from the bog she had walked into with such stupidity.

You thought you were so bloody important, Cassidy Adams, she berated herself. As if you are the only thing capable of making him go quiet and moody and taciturn like this! You jumped to stupid conclusions, and so you ended your pretty affair yourself. You were so frightened that he might hurt you that you took a knife and slashed yourself—as if that way it would hurt less. You could have had tonight with him; you could have had heaven knows how much longer, if only you hadn't been such a self-centred moron!

And so, because she was furious with herself and incapable of facing just how badly she had blundered, she attacked. 'And I suppose you were just going to leave for work as usual tomorrow, and not even tell me about it at all!'

He looked as if the accusation had staggered him. 'Of course I would have told you. I just——' He stopped dead, and it was almost a minute before he said, slowly, as if he knew how feeble it sounded, 'I just didn't want to tell you yet.'

She didn't look at him, and a moment later he left the room. It took him only a few minutes to pack a bag;

she was still standing by the sink, still clutching the towel, when he came back. 'Reid——' she said, uncertainly.

He didn't even break his stride. 'Don't worry, Cassidy. A bargain is a bargain—I'll let you know how the conference comes out.'

And after that, how was she to tell him she was sorry for it all, that she hadn't meant it, and that if it was left up to her she would never want to leave him at all?

So she stood there quietly instead, and watched him go out of her life. Her fingernails clenched against her palms until the skin was lined with ridges, but that was not the worst of the pain; it would pass. The other agony she felt would be with her as long as she lived.

If there had been a reasonable alternative, she would not have stayed at the Cottage at all. But she couldn't bring herself to take Chloe up on her offer; even if there were no other considerations, Cassidy decided, she was in no shape just now to withstand questions, and Chloe would no doubt have plenty to ask. She considered going to a hotel, but concluded that she simply couldn't afford the rates for even a few days. And it looked as if apartment-hunting was going to be more difficult, and more expensive, than she had anticipated.

'You're spoiled, that's all,' she tried to tell herself on Thursday, after she had looked at a couple of apartments on her lunch hour. 'Moving into Mission Hill, even on a very temporary basis, has ruined you for ordinary living!'

But the fact was, the two apartments had been equally impossible, over her budget and located in less-than-likeable neighbourhoods, as well.

So she went back to the Cottage after work, with copies of all the local newspapers under her arm, and, when an hour of telephoning netted her only an aching ear and a very brief list of possibilities for tomorrow's lunch hour, she called a halt to the search and decided to work on her story for a while instead.

It took her mind off the apartment problem, that was for sure; her notes were in such a scrambled mess that it took half an hour to get them all organised again. What on earth had she been thinking of, she wondered, to have shoved them into her briefcase in such disorder? She'd been working on the story just a couple of days ago, and Reid had come into the room unexpectedly, but surely——

Reid—that was it. He must have picked the lock on her briefcase—it wasn't much of a lock; a sharp twist in the right place and it would open—and had a look at her work, and then thrust the pages hurriedly back when he was finished. She tried to work herself into a fury over his snooping and the lack of trust that had led to it, but she couldn't do it. It was scarcely a crime, and though she didn't like the idea of his shuffling through her papers, she certainly understood it. At any rate, she thought with a half-smile, the notes wouldn't do him much good. The half-finished story was what he would really have been interested in, and it hadn't been in the briefcase at all, until she had got it out of her desk drawer today.

She tried to polish the story, smoothing out each sentence, each transition, but with every paragraph she seemed to run headlong into Reid again, and then she would find herself long minutes later, the story forgotten, dreaming of him and how she would have liked things to be. Finally she gave it up altogether and went downstairs to his oak-panelled den and ruthlessly searched his desk until she found the address of the summer house on Table Rock Lake. Fair was fair, she told herself. He'd rummaged through her private pos-

sessions. Besides, she needed that address; she never had
made the apology she owed to his mother.

'That,' she told herself ruthlessly, 'is because you were
hoping to tell Jenna in person how sorry you are to have
believed everything Kent told you, and to have put all
the blame on her. And you were also hoping that circumstances might have been very different by then—that
you and Reid——'

But it hurt too much to think of things like that. It
was just as well, she thought, that she had called a halt
to the whole thing, mistaken though she had been about
the details. For the end had been inevitable, and the pain
would only have been worse if it had been postponed.

And yet, she could not bring herself to wish that it
had never happened. Knowing Reid—loving him—had
been worth it all. And if some day she rewrote the memories a bit and edited out the pain, so that she could
hold the good things that were left close to warm her
heart—well, no one could be hurt by that.

And revising the memories wasn't taking such very
large liberties, after all. There had been something very
special about the way he had treated her and looked after
her and cared for her, and, even if at first it had been
only the baby's welfare he was trying to protect, still he
had cherished Cassidy, as well, in the best sense of the
word. And that kind of caring was what love was all
about, wasn't it?

Love, she thought, was a lot more than acting out
one's physical longings in a sexual way. Love showed up
in the tiny thoughtful things, like searching out fudge
at midnight simply because she craved it. Things like
showing up at a college dance just because she had to
be there, and bringing her blueberry muffins and coffee
in bed . . .

The telephone rang, and she picked it up without a thought.

'You're still there,' Reid said.

Idiot, she told herself. You should have ignored it and let it ring. 'I'll be out tomorrow, I swear——'

'No—that's no problem. It looks as if I might be tied up here for a long time.'

'It isn't going well?'

'It's slow, that's certain. And when you've got sixteen guys locked in a small room and no one has had a shower in three days——'

'Reid, you haven't been there for three days!'

'Well, it feels as if it's been that long. I hate to ask you, Cassidy—but would you mind if I came out to the Cottage for a minute?'

Her hand tensed on the telephone, and then she forced herself to relax. Thank heaven, she thought, that she had answered the phone; otherwise he'd have thought the house empty, and they would both have had an unpleasant surprise. 'It's your house,' she said. 'Of course I don't mind.'

'It may be late,' he warned. 'I left a notebook on my desk, and I'll need it in the morning—but I don't know when we'll actually break up for the night.'

Her hand stretched out almost involuntarily, and caressed the leather surface of a pocket-sized notebook that lay on the corner of the blotter, forgotten. It warmed under her fingertips, almost unnaturally fast, as if it were a part of his body, responding to her touch——

'I could bring it to you,' she said, before she could even think. She caught herself a split second later and added hurriedly, 'I was going out anyway.'

'What on earth for, at this time of night?'

As if it was any of his business, she thought, a little resentfully. Her stomach rumbled, reminding her that she hadn't bothered with dinner. That was it, she thought. 'Because I'm longing for strawberry pie.'

His voice warmed. 'From Delmonico's? That explains it, then. If the notebook wouldn't be too much trouble for you, I'd appreciate it.'

'I'll just leave it at the hotel desk.'

'Cassidy——' He sounded almost hesitant. 'I'd rather you didn't, because it's sort of important. I'll tell them to let you have a key. I'm in suite C on the seventeenth floor.'

She almost argued. But he wouldn't be there, anyway, so what difference did it make whether she went to his room? She wouldn't have to see him——

It makes a lot of difference to me, she thought, as she put the telephone down gently. I want to see him. I want to hold him and kiss that loneliness away——

Lonely? Had he really sounded lonely? Or had she heard that tremor in his voice simply because she wanted so badly for it to be there?

She sat there at his desk for a long time, with her hand resting on the notebook, and when she rose it was with a new sort of resolve—not a girl's rainbow-coloured dreams this time, but a woman's reality. There was nothing to be gained by standing on the sidelines feeling sorry for herself, she decided. If she put herself back in the game, she might indeed be hurt, but pain was an inevitable part of life. What was foolish was to deliberately suffer it before it was required, in an attempt to make it easier to bear.

The Kendrick was one of the city's premier downtown hotels. Reid had explained to her once why he had selected it as a site for the meeting; it was convenient for the out-of-town people, but also it was large enough to be an anonymous setting, where a group could meet without calling undue attention to itself. Such a large group of officials turning up at his office would cause instantaneous tremors through the company, and probably the entire construction industry as well.

His suite was quietly luxurious. She let herself in with the key and stood for a moment just inside the door, listening. But there was no hint of sound, so she almost tiptoed across the living-room, put his notebook down precisely in the centre of the coffee-table, and begun to unpack the brown paper bag she had brought along.

Her preparations took scarcely any time, and after that all there was to do was wait. Before long she was becoming agitated, with nothing to do but think. It had seemed so simple when she'd been out at the Cottage; all she had to do, it had seemed then, was to tell him that she'd been mistaken, and that she wasn't quite ready to leave him after all. But now—the idea of facing him here was almost too much for her. Twice she jumped up from the couch, ready to flee. Twice she forced herself to sit down again.

It was the wee hours of the morning, and the hotel had settled into its night-time hush, when Reid came in. He flipped the lights on and stopped dead in the middle of the doorway.

'Room service,' Cassidy said brightly. He didn't move. 'I thought you sounded as if you'd like some strawberry pie, too...' Her voice trailed off. Was he just going to stand there like a stone? She began again, uncertainly. 'I thought—you said the notebook was important, and so I didn't want to just leave it—— '

'It isn't *that* important,' he said quietly.

So much for your excuses, Cassidy, she told herself. Now is the moment of truth. Tell him why you're really here——

She drew the breath that she would use to apologise, but she couldn't do it. Fear clamped down on her throat, almost choking her, and the words would not come out.

Good grief, she thought, you must look like a fish, opening and closing your mouth with no result! 'Well, now that you've got your notebook——' Then, with relief, she remembered that she did have a legitimate reason for hanging around. 'Oh, you got a phone call just as I was leaving the Cottage. It was a woman's voice, asking for Mr Cavanaugh, and when I asked if I could take a message she just said that she would call again some other time. She was very polite, but she wouldn't give a name.' And I didn't press too hard, Cassidy reminded herself, because I was afraid to find she might be the one who's important to you. And the truth was that I didn't want to let anything get in the way of pulling this foolish stunt. I was so certain it would all come right——

For a moment, Reid didn't seem to hear. 'It wasn't my mother, was it?'

'Does she call you Mr Cavanaugh?' Cassidy asked tartly.

'Not usually.' He shrugged and said, 'So it can't have been very important. Did I hear you say something about strawberry pie?'

'It's in the bag. I'll let you get your rest now.' She didn't look at him as she brushed past.

'Cassidy——' His hand shot out and closed on her arm. 'Stay a while. Please.'

She hadn't imagined it; there *was* a note of loneliness in his voice. She looked up at him, and he stared down into her eyes, took a deep, astonished breath, and pulled her into his arms, almost roughly. His first kiss sent cold shivers darting along each vein, each nerve, but with the second, the cold was banished by liquid fire——

'Stay with me tonight,' he whispered, almost hoarsely. 'I need your warmth close beside me, Cassidy. Just let me hold you tonight——'

She almost started to cry then, with happiness, for surely if it was only physical attraction he felt for her he would not have said it quite that way. And so she gave herself gladly into his care, and told him with every nerve-shattering response her body could give that she was sorry for the mistake she had made.

It was the sound of the suite's door closing that woke her next morning, at an unconscionably early hour. He was already gone, then, she thought, stretching lazily. Back to that closed, smoke-filled room where harsh bargains would be struck today, or tomorrow, or soon. She only hoped that the night had left him as relaxed as she felt this morning.

She wrapped herself in the Kendrick's complimentary bathrobe and rolled up the sleeves to leave her hands free. 'One size fits all,' she muttered. 'What they really mean is that one size fits none!'

A breakfast tray stood almost untouched on the low table by the sofa. Coffee in a thermal server, juice, danish pastry—Room Service had sent enough for two, and they'd even included both the *Alternative* and its morning competitor. She broke off a bite of pastry and reached for the newspaper.

And choked down a scream as she saw her story staring up at her from the most prominent position on page one. Her story, so carefully crafted, so precisely worded, so cautiously protected until the time was right for it to be released. Her story, which she knew without a fragment of doubt was still in her briefcase out at the Cottage. Her story about Reid's new project, crammed full of things Reid had said and facts Reid had shared with her—all given only after her solemn promise that nothing would be released until the project was finalised.

Oh, yes, she thought as her eye ran down the long straight columns of type. It's my story, all right.

Except for one thing; it carried Chloe McPherson's byline.

CHAPTER TEN

THE shock of seeing the story there—where it could not possibly be—paralysed Cassidy, and it was a couple of minutes before she even began to think of the consequences it would have on her, on Reid, on the project itself. But when she did, her head started to pound as if a hundred riveters were taking turns working on her skull.

It was no good pretending to herself that perhaps it would make no difference at all; a copy of that newspaper had been delivered this morning to every room in the hotel. Every one of the fifteen men who had been in that negotiating session last night with Reid had seen the newspaper. And with the big, black headline grabbing for attention, it was a safe bet that none of them had missed the story either. No wonder Reid had lost interest in his breakfast; he had sat there over his coffee and watched all the work, all the planning, all the negotiating, turn into wisps of smoke and blow away. And as for Cassidy's reaction——

She couldn't even draw a deep breath; her chest was too tightly constricted, as if it were her body, and not simply her career, that was being squeezed to a pulp by the press that had printed this particular issue of the *Alternative*. She considered the matter of her job, fleetingly, and dismissed it. It was too late to worry about that; the fact was that a reporter who gave a promise and then broke it would never be trusted again once that word got out. And the news about this would fly; after all the publicity, when the union negotiations fell through and the project died, there would have to be an announcement. She wouldn't blame Reid if he was so angry that he explained precisely what had happened, to anyone who cared to ask——

She wondered, uneasily, exactly what he did think. Did he believe she had done this on purpose, feeding information to Chloe so that her own promise of confidentiality could be maintained, however thin the rationale? The fact that he had not confronted her took on new and ominous implications. She almost wished that he had come storming into the bedroom a few minutes ago and slapped her awake and demanded to know what she was thinking of to have treated him so...

But he had not. He had apparently felt that he already knew everything he needed to know, that talking to her would not clarify the situation.

She read the story through with gritted teeth. It only made her headache worse, for Chloe had not stolen the original version, word for word. Instead, she had used Cassidy's story as a base, adding her own interpretations, speculating in that well-honed way of hers about the reasons behind it all, and hinting, without ever quite saying, that there was something Reid was trying to hide. She must have been working on it for days.

And I, Cassidy thought, have been too absorbed in my own romantic little world for the last week to notice anything unusual going on. What a fool I've been!

She wasted a couple of minutes in feeling sorry for herself, and then she straightened her spine with determination and went to get dressed. Reid might have jumped to the wrong conclusions, but she had to admit he'd had reason. In any case, that did not mean that she didn't owe him—and herself, as well—her best efforts to get the whole mess straightened out.

If, she told herself, it wasn't already far too late to do anything at all.

The first warning that Chloe had of Cassidy's approach was when the morning *Alternative* hit the corner of her desk with a slap that sounded as if a sudden thunderstorm had materialised in the middle of the newsroom. The woman jumped two feet off her chair, and turned white.

Cassidy was grimly glad to see the effect.

'Oh, it's you,' Chloe said. 'What on earth are you thinking of? That sounded like a gunshot, you know.'

'You stole my story,' Cassidy said. She didn't bother to hold her voice down, and for twenty feet around Chloe's desk staff members looked up in surprise.

'What story?'

'This story.' Cassidy thrust the newspaper under Chloe's nose.

Chloe shrugged. 'There's no copyright on ideas, you know. So what if we both started down the same trail, following the same scent?'

'There was no coincidence about it, Chloe!'

The editor's voice cut across the quarrel. 'Don't you think this would be better dealt with in private, both of you?'

'Private?' Cassidy said bitterly. 'You must be kidding, Brian. When you splashed it all over Kansas City without even asking me why I hadn't told you what I was working on, and why it shouldn't be released yet?'

'What *you* were working on? You told me long ago you'd given up on Cavanaugh!'

'Oh,' Cassidy said. 'That explains it, then. She didn't tell you it was my story. I wondered how a professional like you could square it with your conscience to steal one reporter's work, let another put a sensational slant on it, and publish it as gospel truth. Now I know—you're not vindictive, Brian, you're just incompetent!'

His face flushed. 'Come into my office, both of you.'

Cassidy ignored him. She turned to Chloe. 'I told you that I always keep a printed copy of the things I'm working on—so you searched my desk and found it, didn't you? You might as well not bother to deny it— I've got my notes and my own copies, if I have to prove that you stole it.'

'All right,' Chloe said with composure. 'I won't deny that I saw what you'd done. I was looking for a stapler. But when I saw the story, I read it. Then I did some looking into the matter—— '

And found my notes, as well, Cassidy thought. No wonder they were scrambled, though I'd have thought Chloe would be more careful to cover her tracks.

'And the longer I looked, the more it became apparent that you were letting opportunities to break that story go by one after another,' Chloe announced. 'In fact, if it was left to you there would never be a story at all, would there? You weren't covering the news for the paper; you were covering it up for Reid Cavanaugh. For your ex-husband.'

There were a couple of gasps from staff members, most of whom were now unabashedly eavesdropping. Brian said, his voice rising, 'Why haven't I heard that accusation before, Chloe?'

'Because she didn't want you to ask me about it,' Cassidy said flatly. 'I suppose you actually believed that she dug up all that information on her coffee breaks this week!'

'It was obvious what was going on.' Chloe shrugged. 'You wouldn't say where you were living. That made me suspect, of course, and then when you answered the telephone at his house last night——'

The polite request for Mr Cavanaugh, Cassidy thought bitterly. Of course Chloe would have recognised her voice; after all, she had been expecting to hear it.

They never did move into Brian's office; the rest of the whole ugly matter came out in the middle of the newsroom, and that was where Chloe received her termination notice, too, in front of a dozen interested witnesses, from an editor so furious at the full recital of her conduct that he had turned practically purple by the time he managed to tell her she was fired. Chloe gathered up her personal belongings, muttering something about the shame of it that a reporter's job was no longer to dig out the news, wherever it was to be found and no matter how uncomfortable it made the people who were in power.

But finally she was gone, and Brian said, loudly, with a baleful look at the rest of his staff, 'Well, that is that. Let's all get back to work.'

As if, Cassidy thought in disbelief, it was all a textbook exercise after all. As if it didn't really matter.

But as the others scattered, Brian said, more quietly, 'If you'd only told me what you were doing——'

It was no consolation to know that he was right, that if she had followed her own judgement instead of letting Reid persuade her to keep the whole thing secret, even from Brian, this would not have happened. 'Don't start on me, Brian. I may have been a fool, but you were an idiot not to ask questions about where she got all that stuff.' She added, stiffly, 'I'm sorry I said you were incompetent, though.'

'Chloe brought me a story. She had all the background information—I had no reason to question it.' Brian swallowed hard. 'You're right, of course. I should have suspected it couldn't be so smooth.'

'Unfortunately, that doesn't solve the problem, does it?' She pulled her desk drawers open and looked at the mass of personal items that had found their way to the office over the months. 'Do we have a box lying around somewhere?'

'A box? What for——? Cassidy, you aren't going to quit over this, are you?'

'It's no grandstand gesture, Brian, believe me. It's simply practical—who's going to talk to me after this?'

'But it wasn't your fault.'

'Do you actually think anyone's going to believe that? It's sort of my word against Reid's.'

'But if he's really your ex-husband——' Brian stopped. 'Well. Yes. I see. Is there anything I can do to salvage the situation? An editorial, perhaps, apologising for our bad timing——'

She shook her head. 'That would be too late. A personal apology might be in order—the *Alternative* can't exactly afford to go around offending people.'

He sighed. 'It's that important?' He could see the answer in her face. 'All right—a personal apology. If there is any way to get into that meeting, of course.' He sounded as if he hoped there wasn't.

There was. She buttonholed the bellboy who was standing watch outside the small ballroom where the meeting was going on, and told him that it was imperative that they go in, that there was a death message for Mr Cavanaugh. The bellboy took one look at her face and waved them through.

It had been a well-calculated bet, Cassidy thought. The way she looked, no doubt the bellboy would have believed her if she'd said her best friend had just been stepped on by an elephant. Besides, she thought, it was true. There had been a death—the death of all those lovely things she had dreamed last night, when she had believed for a while that everything would be all right . . .

She stopped herself from dwelling on that just in time to face sixteen stony faces, looking up from a long conference table littered with documents and contracts—and newspapers. She didn't even remember what she said, and she didn't really hear Brian, either. She was looking at fifteen strangers and one man who would have been dear and familiar if he hadn't looked so hard, and almost alien—and if the expression in his dark eyes hadn't seemed to say, Is this why you came here last night? Because you wanted one final fling before you betrayed me?

She stopped looking at him then. It was too late, she thought. Too late to save the project—that was apparent from the sixteen men who responded only with silence. And far too late to save any hopes she might have had of living out her own dreams.

The hushed cold of the room sank deep into her body and settled like a bitter weight against her heart. But she left the room dry-eyed, with her head high. This time it hurt far too much for tears to soothe the ache.

She let herself in the back door of the Cottage with a sense of relief. At least here, in the cool quiet dimness, she could be alone for a few minutes, to sort out what had happened, and perhaps to begin to think of the future. She had not gathered up her personal things at the *Alternative* office after all, but it had not been Brian's pep talk which had prevented her from going back and taking care of that detail—just the knowledge that the newspaper was a loose end that could be tied up any time, while the Cottage was a different matter altogether. She had to get her possessions out of the Cottage, and soon.

She would still have to face Reid, of course—much as she wanted to just run away, she couldn't do that this time. For her own sake, she would have to face him and apologise. But it would be far better to do so on neutral ground—not here, where they had shared such passion, and she had nurtured such hopes.

She was so absorbed in her thoughts that she was in the master bedroom before she realised that there was already someone there. She gave a startled little scream, and a woman turned from the bureau along the opposite wall, brandishing a duster.

'Oh—Mrs Miller.' Thanks for the surprise, Reid, Cassidy thought acidly; you could have told me she was coming home! 'I thought you were still at Table Rock.'

The housekeeper shrugged. 'It always takes a week to clean the place up in the spring. As soon as I'm done, I come back.' She did not seem startled or ill at ease at Cassidy's presence.

Cassidy herself didn't have that much poise. She tried to turn her embarrassment into pleasantry. 'Is——? Did Mrs Cavanaugh come back with you?'

The housekeeper shook her head.

That's some relief, Cassidy thought. 'I just came by to pick up some of my things,' she said, trying to sound casual. 'I'll try not to get in your way while I pack.'

Mrs Miller didn't answer. She also didn't offer to leave the room.

Cassidy bit her tongue and pulled a suitcase out from under the bed. I don't blame her, she thought as she began to fold clothes into the case. She's just making sure I don't take anything that isn't obviously mine.

Still, it was a bit embarrassing. Her things had crept into odd corners all over Reid's bedroom. She knew, of course, why that had happened—her unexpressed, deep-down longing not to leave at all. To pretend that this was for always...

Her hands moved mechanically from drawer to suitcase, capturing frilly lingerie and delicate stockings. Some of her things were actually tangled up with Reid's; she tried not to let herself turn pink as she struggled to free them.

Not that Mrs Miller seemed to notice; she was very busy polishing the furniture and cleaning the mirrors. The silence made Cassidy nervous. Anything, she thought, would be better than this.

Finally, she said, 'I never did thank you for making the fudge for me that night.'

Mrs Miller snorted. 'It wasn't me. Now if you want to thank me for cleaning up the mess he left in my kitchen——'

Cassidy's hands stilled on a ruffled peach blouse. 'Reid made it himself?' It startled her, though she supposed it shouldn't have.

'I should say he did. And he didn't even put the dishes to soak, so the next morning I had dried fudge caked in my best saucepan, and all over the counter tops, and dripping on to the floor——'

'Was that where he learned about disposable pans?' Cassidy asked flippantly. It was better, she told herself, than getting sentimental about it. Once, she would have taken it as evidence that he had cared. And perhaps he had—once. Now, she hoped, she was older and wiser, and she knew that it no longer mattered. Too many other things had got in the way.

She finished the first suitcase and started on another. Mrs Miller dusted the bureau for what seemed to Cassidy to be the third time and finally left the room.

Cassidy sighed in relief and got out her almost new box of stationery. It was beginning to look as if the whole thing would be taken up by apologies to the various members of the Cavanaugh family, she thought wryly, and uncapped her pen, sitting cross-legged on the bed with the breakfast tray across her lap.

'Dear Reid,' she wrote, and stopped there. What words were there to tell him how sorry she was about the way the story had turned out? And as for the rest, how could she possibly thank him—as she should, if she was honest—for restoring her to life, and for teaching her not only passion but love, a love she would cherish for the rest of her life?

'Dear Reid—I want to thank you for everything, and to apologise for what must seem a dreadful way to respond to your kindness——' Good grief, Cassidy, she told herself. You are not writing a Victorian novel. She crumpled the page and threw it at the wastepaper basket. It missed.

'Is that another one of your famous farewell notes, Cassidy?' It was almost gentle.

She looked up, hazel eyes wide with shock. The bedroom door closed with a firm click, and Reid leaned against it.

He can't be here, she thought. Unless they all just walked out as soon as Brian and I left, and didn't even bother to talk about it any more. That thought gave her a sick feeling in the pit of her stomach. He hadn't even had a fair chance—and she was the one who had robbed him of it. 'I didn't expect you'd be coming any time soon,' she said quietly, 'so I thought——'

'That much was obvious.' He crossed the room, slowly, as if approaching a wild creature who might bolt and run at any moment. 'You've always been good at leaving, haven't you, Cassidy?' He stooped to pick up the unfinished note, read it, and ripped it firmly into bits. 'It's almost a talent you've got, for always having the last word.'

She sat there quietly in the middle of his bed. He had a right to his anger, after all.

'Why?' he said.

She moved, uneasily. 'I suppose it's because Chloe was jealous—after she left, I got the best assignments, and when she came back, there I was in her place, and I had this story that she would have loved to get, and I wasn't even doing anything with it——'

He shook his head. 'Not the story, Cassidy. The rest of it.' He pointed at the two pieces of luggage, packed and closed and ready to be picked up.

'Why I'm leaving?' She must have sounded surprised. 'It's finished, Reid—it's over.'

'Yes—you told me that a couple of days ago. And yet last night, you came to me.'

'Last night was——' It was beautiful and right and good, and I will treasure that memory for the rest of my life, she thought. And I will not lie about it now, and say it was a mistake. 'You don't need to worry that I'll be hanging around any more or nagging you.'

'You'd like to think that it's over, wouldn't you?' It was almost gentle.

Her breath began to come in short, fast bursts. If he meant—could he mean that it wasn't over between them, that, despite the fiasco with the story, he wasn't waiting impatiently for her to go?

'You've got your story; that's all you cared about,' he said, and the fleeting hope died, stillborn. 'In your own way you're just as ruthless as Chloe is, aren't you?'

'I'm not——' But what difference did it make, what he thought of her, now? Perhaps it was just as well if he thought she had no heart at all; then he wouldn't ever know just how thoroughly he had shattered it.

'I suppose I should be flattered that you considered the story worth so much.' He rubbed the back of his hand along his jaw, as if uncertain whether he had finished shaving that morning.

He was obviously hurting, and she couldn't stand it. 'It wasn't the story,' she said stiffly. 'I wish there hadn't been any damned story!'

'No doubt,' he said, as if it didn't matter. 'But there was, and it's a bit late to change that fact now. Tell me, Cassidy, haven't you considered the possibility that it will never be over?'

'I don't know what you mean——'

'What if you're pregnant?'

She didn't know until then that she had even faced the possibility, or admitted it to herself. But obviously she had; there was no shock in the idea, just a scared, sad little feeling in the pit of her stomach, as if she had gambled against unknown odds, and now she knew she had lost—she was just waiting to find out how severe the loss had been.

'Don't worry about it,' she said. She slid off the bed and stood up. 'Things are different now from how they were with Fudge. If I'm pregnant——'

He said something under his breath.

You've lost your mind, Cassidy, she told herself blankly. Or your hearing suddenly failed. He can't possibly have said what you thought you heard.

'I hope you are,' he repeated. It was louder, and there was a harsh edge to his voice.

She bent to pick up the suitcases. 'If I am, you'll never know.'

'Don't bet on it. I know your tricks now, Cassidy. And this time I will come after you——'

'And take my baby? You wouldn't find it so easy this time, Reid. I'm not desperate, and my baby is not for sale——' She stopped herself, abruptly realising how foolish the whole thing was. To argue over a child that was no more than a hypothetical possibility—how stupid it was! But she couldn't seem to stop herself. 'I suppose you mean that I owe you a healthy baby—a replacement for defective goods——'

His face darkened, and his hands closed on her arms and pulled her upright. 'Don't you ever again imply that Fudge was only a piece of merchandise to me, to be bought and paid for. He was my baby, too, Cassidy—not biologically, but in every way that matters, as much as this child is.'

'*If* there's a child at all,' she reminded, in a brittle voice. 'Lord, I must have been mad to take such a chance—not even to protect myself!'

'Both of us were a little insane, I think,' he said heavily. He turned away from her and crossed the room to throw himself down in the armchair by the bay window.

That was a fair enough appraisal, she thought. I actually allowed myself to believe, deep in the hidden corners of my mind, that if there was a child it would be different this time—that I could have my baby, and Reid, too.

His eyes, disturbingly dark, searched her face. 'I knew there was nothing preventing a pregnancy,' he said, finally, 'and I decided that I didn't care. If a new life resulted from our act of love——'

'Of love?' she said bitterly. She turned her back on that searching stare. 'I don't quite——'

'Then I would welcome that child. For its own sake, and also because at least then you could not walk away from me again as if none of it mattered. You would have to make a choice, then——'

She wheeled to face him. 'What kind of a sadist wishes that sort of pain on people, Reid?'

His eyes were sorrowful. 'I remembered how much it hurt you to think of giving Fudge up—and I knew that you couldn't do it again. And I thought that, even though you weren't willing to make a commitment to me, you would to our child——'

Cassidy's heart was slamming so hard against her ribs that she thought it was going to burst.

'And we could make some sort of bargain between us—a bargain that would let you keep the baby, and let me . . . keep you.' It was no more than a harsh whisper, at the end.

She was staring at him, wide-eyed. Everything seemed to stop, except for the whispering rush of blood in her ears that reminded her she was still alive.

He rubbed his temples. 'Stupid, wasn't it? To think that it could make any difference—that it would be enough——'

Her voice had frozen somewhere deep in her throat. She tried to speak, and only a hoarse croak emerged.

'It was what I'd planned to do when Fudge was born, you see,' he went on quietly. 'I was going to use him to hold on to you, until perhaps you would see that I——' He stopped, and sighed. 'It started—I don't even know when. That first night at the coffee shop, perhaps, when you defied me instead of grabbing at what I offered, as I'd expected you would. By the time I realised it, you'd made your way into my heart and snuggled down to stay. I felt so guilty,' he admitted. 'For wanting to take you into my bed, when I'd promised to protect you. Even just for loving you, when you were still mourning Kent, and carrying his child.' He sighed. 'I knew very well that I could never compete with Kent. Not the reality, I mean—I wouldn't have been half so afraid of that. But your memories of him—idealising him as you did—no living man could stand up to that.'

She shook her head, but she could not express what she meant.

'But I thought that, surely, some day you would begin to get over losing him, and if I could just hold on to you until that day came—— Sometimes I thought it might not be so far away. When you began to laugh again...' He sighed. 'I thought there was time—that when the baby was born, I'd just suggest that you stay a while, and then perhaps as the weeks and the months went by you might come to consider me a substitute...

You? she thought. But you were always so certain of yourself—I never dreamed that you could feel inadequate!

She swallowed the lump in her throat. Her voice was a bare squeak. 'I never, ever considered you a substitute, Reid.'

It seemed to age him. His gaze dropped to the carpet, and he didn't see her hands go out to him. 'But suddenly Fudge was gone, and I wasn't even there to hold you— Not that it mattered; it was obvious that you didn't want me around.'

I thought you didn't want to be bothered, she wanted to scream. I thought that once the baby was gone you'd be eager to get rid of me, to put it all behind you——

'And you went, too,' he said heavily, 'and I never even had a chance to tell you how sorry I was.'

'You didn't try very hard,' she whispered.

Reid's voice sounded strange, as if it had been rubbed with sandpaper. 'You—hoped that I'd look for you?'

She nodded. 'And when you didn't——' Her voice was so low that it hardly disturbed the quiet of the room.

'I told myself that if you wanted to disappear, Cassidy, I had no right to hunt for you, to make you miserable again. But for four years, every street I've walked down, every crowd I've passed through, I have looked for that crown of red-gold hair, and whenever I thought I saw it——' He came up behind her, very quietly, and his hand brushed against a lock of hair that had tumbled over her shoulder. His fingertips trembled a little. 'Cassidy——'

She turned to him, blinding-hot tears blurring the hazel of her eyes. 'You were right, Reid. Everything you said to me, about how I was afraid to live, afraid to love again. But it wasn't losing Kent that did that to me—or even losing Fudge. It was losing you.'

He pulled her tight against his chest, and buried his face in her hair. She was safe there in his arms, and warm, and her hands clutched almost convulsively on his shirt, as if someone might seek to pull her away.

'I fought so hard to keep from falling in love with you,' she whispered. 'It was disloyal to Kent! But I think I knew, the night Fudge got his name—that it was you...' She sniffed.

'I thought you were crying because Kent wasn't there,' he confessed unsteadily. 'Because it was only me instead.'

She shook her head. 'No. Oh, no.'

'Why did you run away?'

'Because I couldn't bear to wait till you told me to go——'

'I never would have, Cassidy.'

She shook her head. 'I was afraid of that, too, I suppose. You were so blasted kind to me—kind, and nothing more. I didn't want your pity——'

'Is that why you wouldn't let me help you? Why you insisted on paying that money back?'

'I didn't want your money, Reid. And what I did want, I didn't think I could have. I wanted your love—I wanted you to treasure me for myself...' Her voice died, choked with the memory of that desperate longing.

'I did,' he whispered. 'And I always shall. Lord, how I love you, Cassidy! It's torn me apart this last week, trying not to frighten you away again—trying to show you what we could have together, and yet give you room, and time——'

'All the room and the time that I didn't need,' she said. 'And all the while, I was trying to pretend that it wouldn't break my heart to walk away from you, my love.'

'What fools we've been,' he said. 'Both of us, too afraid to take a chance, and tell the truth...'

And then, for a long time, they didn't talk at all. There were things that could not be said in words, that could be communicated far better in the language of touch, of kisses, of healing tears.

Finally, Reid put his cheek down against her hair— she was sitting on his lap by then, in the big armchair—and said, unsteadily, 'I've been so afraid, Cassidy. Afraid to trust my heart, which said you couldn't act that way unless I meant something to you. Terrified that the logical explanation was the right one instead, and that it was only the story you really wanted——'

'Story?' she murmured. 'What story?'

'The one you're going to write for tomorrow's *Alternative* about the new variety of Cavanaugh condos.'

She snuggled her head deeper into his neck. 'I'm not sure I still work for the *Alternative*, Reid——' Then she heard him, belatedly. 'Do you mean it didn't fall through? I thought it must have, or you couldn't have got here so quickly—— '

'Most of the shouting was over by the time you and your tame editor popped in. I won't pretend the story this morning didn't cause a problem, but eventually the consensus was that no damned newspaper was going to keep a whole bunch of national unions from doing whatever they pleased——'

'Chloe would be mortified,' Cassidy murmured. She sat up, reluctantly. 'I'd better get to work, then.'

'There's plenty of time. Have I told you that I love you?'

'Not in the last five minutes or so.'

He smiled down into her eyes, and kissed her, a long and leisurely caress. Cassidy decided, a little dizzily, that he was right—there would be plenty of time later to work.

'Stupid fool that I am,' he said thoughtfully. 'Expecting that you'd know by osmosis, or something, when I think I've told everyone else that I love you. My mother included. I should have listened to her—she was so convinced everything would work out that she's already arranged to move out of the Cottage.'

'She told me.' And I was so paranoid, Cassidy thought, that I jumped to all kinds of strange conclusions.

'She's thrilled at the prospect of grandchildren.'

It sent a little shiver of fear to Cassidy's heart. 'Reid,' she said. It was quiet, and almost sad. 'What if I can't carry a baby to term? What if what happened to Fudge happens again?'

'Do you really think that would make me love you less?' He stroked her hair and pulled her even closer. 'Don't be a little fool. It won't happen again, anyway. It wasn't your fault, so there's no reason on earth we can't have, oh, an Olive, perhaps—I can imagine you craving those things by the gallon. Or a Cashew—didn't you tell me once how much you like those? And perhaps a Liverwurst-on-Toast, for good measure——'

'Hush,' she whispered. 'The only thing I'm craving right now is you.'

'Good,' he said huskily. 'I can handle that.'

So Cassidy promptly forgot the whole nonsensical conversation; there were, after all, much more interesting things to think about.

It's a matter of record, by the way, that when their baby girl was born, they named her Shannon Elizabeth.

But her father nearly always called her Muffin.

HARLEQUIN
Romance®

**This September, travel to England
with Harlequin Romance
FIRST CLASS title #3149,
ROSES HAVE THORNS
by Betty Neels**

It was Radolf Nauta's fault that Sarah lost her job at the hospital and was forced to look elsewhere for a living. So she wasn't particulary pleased to meet him again in a totally different environment. Not that he seemed disposed to be gracious to her: arrogant, opinionated and entirely too sure of himself, Radolf was just the sort of man Sarah disliked most. And yet, the more she saw of him, the more she found herself wondering what he really thought about her—which was stupid, because he was the last man on earth she could ever love....

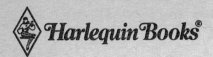
Harlequin Books®

GREAT NEWS...

HARLEQUIN UNVEILS NEW SHIPPING PLANS

For the convenience of customers, Harlequin has announced that Harlequin romances will now be available in stores at these convenient times each month*:

Harlequin Presents, American Romance, Historical, Intrigue:

> May titles: April 10
> June titles: May 8
> July titles: June 5
> August titles: July 10

Harlequin Romance, Superromance, Temptation, Regency Romance:

> May titles: April 24
> June titles: May 22
> July titles: June 19
> August titles: July 24

We hope this new schedule is convenient for you.

With only two trips each month to your local bookseller, you'll never miss any of your favorite authors!

*Please note: There may be slight variations in on-sale dates in your area due to differences in shipping and handling.

HDATES-RR

*Applicable to U.S. only.

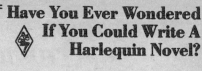

Have You Ever Wondered If You Could Write A Harlequin Novel?

Here's great news—Harlequin is offering a series of cassette tapes to help you do just that. Written by Harlequin editors, these tapes give practical advice on how to make your characters—and your story— come alive. There's a tape for each contemporary romance series Harlequin publishes.

Mail order only

All sales final

Harlequin Superromance®

Available in Superromance this month
#462—STARLIT PROMISE

STARLIT PROMISE is a deeply moving story of a
woman coming to terms with her grief and gradually
opening her heart to life and love.

Author Petra Holland sets the scene beautifully, never
allowing her heroine to become mired in self-pity. It
is a story that will touch your heart and leave you
celebrating the strength of the human spirit.

Available wherever Harlequin books
are sold.

STARLIT-A